Abused and Abandoned

JOYCE MAYO

Manufactured in the United States of America.

Published by Taevo Publishing, Norfolk, VA 23502. Second edition.

Visit our website at www.taevopublishing.com for more information about the author and resources pertaining to abuse.

Cover photography by Veronica J. Garcia
Edited and designed by Tamara Mayo

ISBN: 978-0-9889082-5-3

DEDICATION

This book is dedicated to the memory of my mother, Annie Mae Collington Richardson, and to my father, James Therium Richardson. I thank you for your inspiration. May you both continue to rest in peace.

A special thanks to Tamara Evon Mayo and Taevo Publishing for bringing this story back to life.

Special appreciation to my husband, Dexter Levon Mayo, Sr. May you continue to rest in peace, my love. Also love and thanks to my son, Dexter Levon Mayo, Jr.

CONTENTS

Introduction i

Chapter One 1

Chapter Two 4

Chapter Three 10

Chapter Four 13

Chapter Five 15

Chapter Six 20

Chapter Seven 22

Chapter Eight 24

Chapter Nine 27

Chapter Ten 31

Chapter Eleven 34

Chapter Twelve 38

Chapter Thirteen 40

Chapter Fourteen 42

Chapter Fifteen 47

Chapter Sixteen 51

Chapter Seventeen 54

Chapter Eighteen 58

Chapter Nineteen 63

Chapter Twenty 67

Chapter Twenty-One 71

Chapter Twenty-Two 75

Chapter Twenty-Three 77

INTRODUCTION

Tunisia is the beautiful Black mother of a teenage daughter named Aja. This book is a detailed description of Tunisia's heart-to-heart conversation with her daughter about relationships.

This book is not for the timid. Tunisia graphically recounts the physical and sexual abuse that she and four of her best girlfriends suffered as teenagers.

In an attempt to make her daughter aware of how to avoid being abused in a relationship, the protagonist offers teenage mothers and daughters the warning signals of an abusive person, as well as the alternatives that can and must be taken to avoid becoming another statistical victim.

In case you have already experienced abuse, please know that help is available. Some of these resources are listed at the end of this book. In addition to finding help, I hope that you will also, with the help of God, find hope.

CHAPTER ONE

The decision had finally been made. We'd considered the alternatives, but I decided that this was the only feasible choice. We talked about what was right and what was wrong. We discussed morals and debated over values. It didn't matter what was said. My mind was made up, and the wheels of change were set in motion. I had to act quickly.

My heart was as dark and cloudy as the stormy March weather. The sun was held at bay by the prevailing dark clouds. The trees gave way to the roaring, chilly winds. I rode beside my mother in stubborn silence.

The decision I made had put some distance in our relationship. She had made it clear that she did not agree with my decision. It was the pain that silenced her. She could neither look me in the eye nor speak to me. I thought about writing a book called "The Longest Ride", because the short distance seemed like an eternity.

We pulled into the parking lot of the blue marble building. The old car continued to sputter and rattle several minutes after the ignition was turned off. We were poor, but proud. I cautiously got out of the car and slowly proceeded to the entrance of the clinic.

Mother uttered one final plea: "It's not too late to change your mind. You can cancel this whole ordeal."

The look I gave her told her that I wanted to continue as planned. I somehow wanted to convince her that I knew what I had decided was wrong, and that I would probably regret it for the rest of my life.

We approached a winding staircase leading to the second floor of this building. Upon reaching the top, I heard the grating sounds of machines in the back of the building. We were greeted at the entrance by a mature looking woman. She asked our names, checked the list, and told us to be seated.

The walls of the waiting area were a bright mauve color. A matching shag carpet covered the concrete floor. Beautiful pictures of swans blanketed walls resembling botanical gardens, due to the flowery design of the wallpaper. The peaceful ambience of the room stealthily masked its true purpose.

The oak coffee tables contained an abundance of reading material to distract us from the hard, cold folding chairs. The discomfort of the seats didn't bother me, since it was almost impossible to remain seated for more than a few minutes.

The women sitting in the waiting room varied in age. Some were crying profusely. Some were reading magazines. Others carried on conversations to pass the time away.

I was in a state of shock. I didn't know how to act. I didn't know if I should be sad, mad, or happy. I knew, however, that this was certainly not a dream. Instead, it was a nightmare that had become a reality. I kept wishing I could open my eyes and this terrible ordeal would be over. But I couldn't, and it wasn't.

I asked myself over and over how I got into this situation. It seemed like one day I was going to my classes, then the next day I was going through this... madness. One moment I was bathing in an ocean of ecstasy and in the next, I was drowning in my own tears of sadness. Why hadn't I just listened to my mother?

As I assured myself that this would not happen again, I discreetly scanned the room for a familiar face. My eyes lit up with interest when I spotted a girl from my high school math class.

Her name was Venice. Her eyes were puffy and red as cherries from crying. I felt a little more comfortable knowing that someone in my peer group was going through the same thing as me. Misery really does love company. Our eyes met and she motioned for her mother to follow her over to where we were sitting.

As our mothers introduced themselves, Venice said, "Tunisia, what are you doing here?"

I thought to myself, "What a dumb question...", but before I could respond, her mother snapped, "Girl, the same reason you're here."

Venice and I just sighed and looked down at the floor with embarrassment. We were so hurt and ashamed over this whole situation. My mother just looked at me and disappointedly shook her head, probably wondering where she went wrong.

I would have never thought Venice would be there. She was always perfect. Straight A's, cheerleading captain, and she was voted most likely to succeed. She was president of the student body and editor of the school newspaper.

Venice was one of those upper-class girls who lived in the illustrious part of town. Her parents were very successful. However, I quickly realized that no one's socio-economic background mattered in a place like this. This could happen to any woman.

I quickly started thinking about my own reputation. What if people found out? What if Venice went back to school running off at the mouth? I wouldn't be able to face anyone. Surely, she couldn't be that stupid, I figured. If she told them about me, then she would have to admit that she was here, too.

I guess that question was bothering her too, because almost as if she were reading my mind, she said, "Tunisia, I don't want anyone to know about this. I won't tell if you won't."

We swore each other to secrecy as I inwardly breathed a sigh of relief. Thank goodness! No person on earth (besides the ones in this room with me) would ever know.

Now that my secret was going to be protected, I decided that when this ordeal was over and done with, I would completely erase it from my mind. It would be hard to do, but I had to try. I had no choice.

CHAPTER TWO

In the back row of the waiting room, two white girls were talking about how many times they had been there. Perhaps bragging was the better word. One of the girls boasted that she'd been there four times, not showing any remorse whatsoever.

She even had the audacity to explain the horrifying details. I didn't want to hear any of it. I just wanted everything to be over as painlessly and quickly as possible.

It seemed as though all of the cards were stacked against me, and this was the only way out. While I sat in the rock-hard chair, I thought several times about getting up and leaving, but something kept me anchored to that chair. I just couldn't shake the feeling that this was my only way out.

I tried to think rationally about it, but to no avail. Life is so strange. The same things that make you laugh and smile are the same things that make you cry. How could I know that all of the happiness that I once experienced could turn into such sadness? How could I know that everything was mere lies? How would I be able to know that my world would come crashing down? How could I go on living?

A man wearing a white uniform came out to get the forms. He was a clean-cut, bearded gentleman that walked with a slight limp, yet had an air of confidence. I was hoping he would call my name next, so I could leave that awful place. Instead, he called on the girl who had been there four times.

I was amazed at how many people were there. Who would have thought that this place even existed? The room was buzzing with the chatter of a cocktail lounge. However, Venus and I didn't utter a word.

The conversations ranged from: "My mother said I should never trust a procedure like this," to "My mother demanded that I do this." It didn't matter what our beliefs or reasons were; we were all about to make one of the most serious decisions of our lives.

My mother initially refused to fill out the permission form. I threatened that if I didn't get it done there, I would have to go somewhere else, and the other places may not be as safe as Crestview. In fact, there were many unsafe and illegal clinics around.

Some girls were so afraid to tell their parents about their situations that they would put their lives in extreme risk to get the procedure done. Some of the girls died on the operating tables in those illegal clinics, due to quacks using dirty instruments and rusty tools for surgery. Many bled to death, found several days later on the very same operating tables.

Those "doctors" weren't doctors; they were butchers. Most of the time they wouldn't get caught because they would quickly abandon their businesses, then set up the illegal operation elsewhere.

It wasn't like that at Crestview. There, the surgeries were safe and legal. The operations were performed by professionals that understood all the risks of such a procedure. But at this point, it's time to call it like it is, to say the dreaded word instead of dancing around the issue with words like "operation" and "procedure". I was there to get an abortion.

My mother finally conceded to my demands. I can only assume she was worried about my safety. After hearing all of the horror stories about girls too afraid to tell their parents, and their horrific outcomes, my mother reluctantly signed the forms.

Our relationship wasn't always this strained. We were basically a happy family, but I can pinpoint the day it all started to go wrong. That fateful day in the park where I grew up.

All of the handsome Black brothers came to our park to play basketball. The neighborhood sistas would gladly sit or stand around the court to watch them play, hoping to catch the attention of a cute player.

On one particular day I saw the most beautiful man on two legs. He definitely aroused my curiosity. He was tall and dark-skinned, with a body that looked like steel. I always thought the blacker the berry, the sweeter the juice. He had dark, wavy hair and cat-like hazel eyes.

As he dribbled the ball down the court, sweat poured from his forehead. He jumped as high as the sky and made the rim shudder when he jammed the ball through the hoop. He was fine, and he could jam. He scored fifteen points before the other team even removed their sweats.

The game had finally ended. Some of the brothers went inside the recreation center to change their clothes. When they came out, they looked even sexier in their sweats. Some of the men started to fire up marijuana cigarettes. The smoke-filled air was so thick that it was intoxicating.

He must have been checking me out too, because he walked straight over to me. I was elated. Out of all the sisters out there, he came over to rap to me. There he was, standing right in front of me. I almost couldn't believe my eyes.

I acted like I wasn't nervous, but I was. Every muscle in my body was already pulsating, and I had to tell myself several times to stay cool. I was used to being hit on by handsome men, so this was nothing new.

"I don't really come here to play ball," he grinned widely as his eyes took in my curves. "I come out here to see that bad body of yours."

I sent a flirty little smile back, knowing he was right about my body. I had blossomed into a woman with a very shapely figure. In fact, most men called me a "brick house". Definitely a winning hand. I was only fifteen, but looked like a woman of twenty-one. Most men had no idea I was so young.

That day, I was sporting an eight-inch afro draped in African beads. Large, gold hoops dangled from my ears. My cheekbones sat high on my smooth, dark-skinned face. My body was firm at approximately 110 pounds. It seemed like I had everything going for me – the pretty face, lovely smile, a body that would make a grown man cry. I had everything... except brains.

Things were rough in the 'hood. It was hard for anyone to make it. The only people who seemed to be doing well were the drug dealers, prostitutes, and those involved in other illegal activities. The low-income people didn't have a chance, and the average, working-class people were just getting by.

The system hurt the working-class because they were too rich to be poor, but too poor to be rich. Many were disqualified from receiving assistance because they were five or ten dollars over the limit. Every day was a constant struggle.

My pops was in the military, but it was hard to support a family of seven as a third-class in the Navy. Our income was low enough to qualify for the parks, though. Nowadays, they're referred to as "housing projects" or "the ghetto", but when we were growing up, we lived in "the park". Those low-income apartment buildings were roach-city, and the spray that the housing authority used never worked. The roaches had become immune to it.

We had moved from Rhode Island because the naval bases there were closing down. All of the military personnel and their families were transferred to Norfolk, VA or other states that had naval bases.

As a result, Navy housing was difficult to come across with so many families competing for limited space. It would take two to three years to get into navy housing. Norfolk was a more happening place than Rhode Island, though. There were so many exciting things to see and do.

Museums, theatres, malls, beaches, amusement parks... the list goes on and on. My after-school days and weekends were filled with those activities, along with trips to air shows, historical monuments, and checking out different military bases.

We lived close to the base, so it wasn't hard to jump on the shuttle bus to see the ships, submarines, airplanes, and helicopters. Our parents allowed us to go anywhere on the base, except the clubs and the Strip. We were Navy brats, but we were too grown for our own good.

We never listened to our parents; we always had to find the answers ourselves. We knew we weren't allowed to walk the Strip, yet we did it anyway. Go-Go bars, X-Rated movies, nude bars, porno shops... a lot of adult activities were operating there, but we didn't fully understand the danger.

The basketball court in the park was kind of like our "headquarters", though. It was the place to see and be seen, where everyone could meet someone new. But after seeing and talking to that gorgeous man, I was only interested in getting to know him. So, I would hit the court every weekend, secretly watching him watch me.

I didn't see him at the basketball court one day. The thought of not seeing him was frightening, as well as surprising. I didn't expect to miss him that much, considering he'd only said one sentence to me up to that point.

The regulars were already on the court and picking their teams. The sistas were standing around smoking or corn-rowing different dudes' hair. Usually, the brothers would bring Styrofoam coolers filled with wine bottles of T.J. Swann, Thunderbird, Ripple, or Boone's Farm. They had a routine of smoking a joint or two before the game started. And everyone smoked Kool cigarettes.

The rec center's parking lot was filled big bodied Cadillacs, gleaming Rivieras and El Dorados with the diamond in the back. If the brothers weren't on the court, they were either shooting craps, playing cards, or running women. You could hear people talking about what number they played, and how much money "such-and-such" won.

Then I saw him pull up in his gold Mustang. He started running because he knew he was late and the game was getting ready to start. Even in a rush, he looked damn good. He already knew what team to join because they always held a place for their star player. As he ran by, he winked and gave me a big grin.

It was definitely a great day to be outside. The sun was out and the park was bright. Sounds were coming from everywhere. You could hear "Let's Get It On" by Marvin Gaye coming from one direction and Minnie Ripperton's "Back Down Memory Lane" from another. The recreation center was our rite of passage.

Before showing up at the center, the sistas took extra care to make sure their hair was fixed and looking G-O-O-D. We had it going on with our Afro puffs, false-eyelashes, bell-bottomed slacks, halter tops, platform shoes, and chokers around our necks. And we always wore our mood rings.

Everyone usually met at the basketball court around six o'clock. We loved watching the brothers battle for the right to be called the best. But all I really cared about was my man. Though we technically weren't dating yet, in my mind he was already mine. He was graceful, yet powerful. Fast as a cheetah and he looked as good as gold.

Looking back now, I can remember my grandma saying, "Everything that glitters is not gold!" I'd always wondered what she meant by that. Little did I know that I would soon find out!

He was everything that a woman could want in a man. But could I be enough woman for him? Was there already someone special in his life? Was he married? Single? And if he was single, what kind of woman was he looking for?

Those were the questions that stayed on my mind. I knew it was wrong to lust over a man, but I couldn't help it. The boys that I went to school with just didn't interest me. They seemed so young and immature. They would walk down the hall and pull our hair or give us love taps. So boyish compared to the men on the court.

I wondered how to approach this man that I couldn't keep my eyes off of. Should I tell him that I just turned fifteen, or should I lie and say that I'm older? What did I need to do to let him know I was interested in him? All of these questions rambled on and on in my head. I was thinking so hard that I didn't even notice that the game was about to end. His team had won.

After he changed back into his sweats, imagine my elation when he invited me to his Mustang. The car must have had five coats of turtle wax, because it was gleaming in the sun. I could actually see my reflection on the hood. His car looked clean enough to eat off of, and his rims were squeaky clean. He took good care of his ride, telling me that he used glass cleaner to make the rims shine.

He opened the passenger door, and I took that as my cue to get in. The leather bucket seats swallowed my body, and the car had a fragrance of jasmine. He put his sneakers in the trunk and slipped on some Stacy Adams dress shoes. He opened the driver's side door and slid in.

He reached into the glove compartment, pulled out a Commodores tape and popped it into the eight-track player. "Brick House" started blaring from his speakers, and we shared a smile as his eyes scanned my body again. He had a bad speaker system, because the sound was even vibrating the air.

Sweat was falling from his forehead. I saw some tissues on his dash, so I took one out of the box and wiped the sweat from his skin. He flashed that sexy smile at me again as a way to say thanks.

He asked my name, and I coyly replied, "Tunisia."

He told me his name was Deandre, but I could call him Dee. Then he reached into his cooler and pulled out a bottle of T.J. Swann. He poured us both a paper cup full. The wine was nice and cold.

I didn't care that it was wrong to drink at fifteen; I did it anyway. My parents did their best to raise me right, but I was too grown. I always thought that they didn't know what time it was, and that they were old-fashioned. I told them that their generation was different from mine. Looking back, if I had listened to them, I probably would have saved myself a lot of grief.

Dee and I talked in his car for over two hours. I finally got answers to all the questions rattling around in my mind. His full name was Deandre Lewis and he was stationed in Norfolk for a three-year tour.

He was originally from Philadelphia, and had been in the Marine Corps for a year. He told me he lived on base housing, was very single, and had no plans to get married. Dee stated that if the military wanted him to have a wife, they would have issued him one. He believed it would be too hard to be married while in the service.

He always looked so good in his nicely pressed uniform. His black shoes were polished and shined, and his pants had hard creases down the middle. His white gloves were always spotless.

Dee had guard duty on alternating weekends, making it hard to see him as much as I wanted. However, he said to call him as much as I wanted, and that if he wasn't there to leave a message. He assured me that his fellow Marines would give him the message.

CHAPTER THREE

The man in the white uniform returned to the waiting area, looking for his next subject to open up.

"Tunisia Prentiss... Tunisia Prentiss... go to room number eight!" he shouted.

Tears swelling in my eyes, I looked at my mother, then at Venice. My mind was foggy as I took baby steps towards room number eight. I could hear my heart racing faster and pounding harder. I was very afraid, and wished my mother could be with me. However, the rules didn't allow our mothers or anyone else to be with us in the operating room.

Room Eight had a bed, a machine that looked and sounded like a vacuum cleaner, and some other surgical gadgets. I barely had enough time to slip on the white gown before the doctor entered. He sat down across from me and promptly explained the procedure, then the aftercare process. Then he asked the anesthesiologist to prepare the medication.

A few moments later, the anesthesiologist returned. He injected the medicine into my system and told me to start counting backwards from 100. I made it to 93 and was out like a light.

When I woke up, the ugly procedure was over. I made it through the surgery, but emotionally I felt numb. As they moved me to the recovery section, the doctor said that it had been a boy. How dare he?!

I didn't want to know, but it was too late. That information was branded on me, and I immediately started thinking about what my son might have been when he grew up. Who knows? I would never know, and neither would the world. My numbness was slowly being replaced with guilt.

There were several other girls in the room. All of us were lying in our beds staring at the ceiling. We started talking about how we felt concerning what we'd just been through. We also talked about right or wrong, good decisions versus bad ones.

One girl ruthlessly commented that she was glad it was over. Another girl said she had wanted to keep her baby, but her mom told her that she was a mere baby herself. Her mother didn't think a thirteen-year-old could raise a baby by herself.

I didn't make any comments. I just wanted to forget the whole thing. An hour had passed, and the doctor finally released us from the clinic's care. Before we got up, he asked if anyone had been in pain.

The other girls said no. However, I asked the doctor if he could prescribe some pain pills for me. He wrote me a prescription for infection and pain, then I was released back into the custody of my mother.

Reality struck my mind like a rock hammer. In my heart, I felt like what I had done was wrong. I started thinking that I should have carried my baby and just given him away for adoption. There are so many women in the world that can't have children. They would have been grateful to have the baby. My baby…

He could have been a doctor, or the next president. He could have been anything, yet I destroyed it. I began to cry, the tears stubbornly refusing to stop. They flowed like a river, shaking my body with sobs.

I wished I had listened to my mother. I felt so guilty for what I'd done. I thought about the Ten Commandments my Sunday school teacher made us recite over and over. "Thou shalt not kill" kept reverberating through my head.

That was exactly what I'd done. I had taken a life. I couldn't erase the thought, just like I couldn't take back the decision I made. The guilt continued to mount. I felt like I was losing my mind.

I tried to ease the mental and emotional burden by convincing myself that I did the right thing. I told myself that if I'd kept the baby, I would have been just like the girl around the corner. Her baby always had a messy diaper, and constantly cried and fussed.

That girl never had time for her baby because she was always running the streets. She forced her mother to baby-sit, since she was always partying somewhere. Her mother spent more time with that baby than she did.

We found out later that it was an incest baby. That girl had wanted to abort the pregnancy, but she was too far along. She had been abused, then forced to stare at the result of that abuse every day. Her way of dealing with it was to not deal with it.

I wanted to cry out and explain what I was feeling to my mother. I had been so defiant and hurt her so badly, now I was too embarrassed to speak to her. The ride home went in slow motion. It felt like it took longer getting home than to the clinic.

Mom was still clearly upset; she clutched the steering wheel tightly, her eyes fixed straight on the road ahead. I broke the silence (and my internal madness) by popping a tape into Dad's old eight-track player. Barry White's romantic baritone began to croon, "I've Got So Much To Give".

I became a little more relaxed. I was hearing one of my favorite songs. I started grooving to the music, but my silent duet with Barry was interrupted by my mother's stern lecture.

"You were so damned foolish… acting so impulsively. You should be ashamed of yourself, girl… shouldn't have even been messing with him."

Shooting a quick glare my way, she continued, "Chile, you are just too grown. All he did was use you. I ought to have him arrested."

I drowned out my mother's voice by focusing on the music. I didn't want to hear any of it. What did she know anyway? I knew I'd never be able to live this down, no matter how hard I worked to redeem myself.

She just kept rambling on and on about how she and my dad were trying to do their best to raise all of us kids. She kept condemning me for everything I had done, never letting up on me.

I got so tired of her fussing at me that I finally turned to her and said, "Mom, I wasn't foolish. I was just in love. How was I supposed to know all of this was going to happen? He said he loved me, too."

But I was a fool. Dee had blown my mind. If he told me to jump, I would ask how high and how many times. I really thought that I had something good. Even at fifteen, I believed I was mature enough to handle a relationship. Boy was I wrong!

When we make mistakes, we always ask ourselves, "Why do parents know everything?" It never makes sense until we become parents ourselves. But when I was a kid, I felt like my parents were disconnected from the current trends. After all, it was the seventies. Things were different when my parents courted in the forties and fifties, right?

We finally arrived at our house. Our home. No matter how bad the park looked, it was our home: a place to relax, a place to call our own, a place where you could be surrounded by love.

The other members of the family didn't know what had taken place. It was a tightly-wrapped secret. Everything was going to return to normal… or would it? How could I go on living, knowing what I'd done? Only a Higher Power and time could heal this wound.

When I returned to school, I was still out of it. I was confused and depressed. Venice finally returned to school after a long, serious depression. When I asked her about it, she said that she was trying to forget that tragic episode in her life.

CHAPTER FOUR

Before that awful part of my life, Dee and I had big plans. We were inseparable. When you saw me, you saw Dee. We went everywhere together, and we did everything together. We wanted each other so much. Everything was beautiful, and he was like a dream come true.

I remember at the end of the summer of '70, he gave me a .75 carat diamond ring. And it was the real thing. He said that he wanted to profess his love to me. By that time, we had been going together for about eight months.

Dee would usually pick me up at about six in the evening. We'd spend time at the movies, go to the beach and dinner theatres, and explore new places. He loved the museums and art shows, and he taught me about many artifacts and paintings. Life was good. I couldn't have asked for anything better.

I started babysitting in the 'hood. I liked making my own money to buy things for myself. The woman I babysat for was very kind. She had been married to an alcoholic junkie that wouldn't work or look for a job. His only source of income was selling the household appliances to support his drug habit.

Her name was Leslie, and she had to make it for herself and her children. She separated from him when he started taking her paycheck and physically abusing her. She moved into the 'hood because she couldn't afford better. She also had to apply for food stamps and other public assistance.

Leslie told me that she quit working because they kept cutting her check and food stamps when she got too much money from a job. So she did what she could to get money on the side, making sure it stayed under the table.

She also confided that her husband would sometimes find out where she was. When that happened, he would beat her and steal anything that wasn't nailed down to support his habit. Back then, the police usually didn't intervene, calling them "domestic disputes". They would only offer to take her to the hospital or courthouse to take out a warrant.

Leslie never stayed home. She always said she was working. She never told me where she was employed, but she worked a lot of hours. I was over her house more than I was at my own. I didn't mind though, because many times she would buy me an outfit or two since I took such good care of her children. One thing I noticed: when I cleaned her place, I never saw a pay stub.

I told Leslie that I had a friend and asked if he could come by while I was babysitting. She was cool with it, which I was happy about. It meant Dee and I could spend even more time together.

He would always come over with a bottle of Wild Irish Rose, some R&B tapes, and a few joints. We would wait for the children to go to sleep, then sneak out on the back step to smoke them.

It was wonderful to have him around. He made me feel like a grown woman. He showed me things I never knew existed, and at fifteen, I believed that he taught me how to love and be loved.

The only thing I didn't understand was why I was constantly unable to reach him when I called. It bothered me and stayed on my mind, and I kept asking him about it. He always replied that his schedule was sporadic and he never knew when he would or wouldn't be at the barracks.

The questions would erase from my mind the moment he got close and embraced me. Being next to him made me ache with lust. Whenever he touched me, it was like my body was on fire. His love always took me to paradise, and every time he kissed me, he said I tasted just like candy.

We would listen to Minnie Ripperton when we made love. To me, it always felt deep and passionate, like we were one. Meant to be that way forever, since we were constantly loving each other over and over again.

It seemed as though it would never end, but it did. He always had to meet some type of curfew at the barracks. He would always leave so quickly after we were done making love. I would feel lonely and a little neglected when he left, but pushed those feelings aside.

I found something good. Something that would last forever. I couldn't wait to tell my partners, Avalon and Mecca. They lived in the park too, and were my closest friends.

CHAPTER FIVE

Avalon was a slim, petite light-skinned girl. She wore her long, sandy brown hair in tight cornrows that went past her shoulders. She had features that resembled Vanessa Williams, and she was always well dressed, even though she was from a poor family.

Her stepfather was a military man. All eight of the children had different biological fathers, but he cared for them as if they were his own. But he was very strict and never allowed Avalon to go anywhere. And he treated her very badly when her mother wasn't around.

Avalon still managed to keep a boyfriend named Freddie. Mainly because she was a chronic liar. You could never figure out when she was telling the truth, because she would look you right in the eye and make up a story without flinching.

Just like how she swore that she and Freddie weren't doing anything. Nobody believed her, though. After all, most of the kids in school were having sex. Besides, Freddie was telling his friends that they were doing it. Every time Avalon said she was a virgin, me and Mecca would bust up laughing.

Mecca was a thick, brown-skinned girl. She had one of those Coke bottle figures – heavy on the top and bottom, but thin in the middle. Her pretty face reminded people of Aretha Franklin, and she had a well-kept curly Afro.

Mecca was one of the smartest girls in school. Her only flaw was the old-fashioned, out-of-date clothing she wore. It wasn't her fault, though. Her family was even poorer than Avalon and mine's.

Her father had problems holding down a job. He worked construction whenever he was able to find work, but it seemed like the moment he found a job, he was laid off again. For years he tried, but I guess he got tired of feeling like a failure in front of his large family.

He eventually left his family. He claimed that they would do better without him, and that government assistance could provide better than he could. Mecca had six younger brothers and sisters, all of them from different fathers. Mecca and her youngest brother were his only biological children.

Mecca was very upset when her father left. She drew closer to her mother during the following months. They both tried to compensate for the loss by giving a little extra to each other. Mecca was more obedient and her mother less strict.

Mecca received more liberty to come and go as she pleased, but with one main condition. Her mother made it clear that good hygiene and top-notch education would not be compromised. She was serious about that, and constantly preached, "We may be poor and Black, but we are clean and intelligent."

Mecca taught me a lot about life. Her mother put her on birth control pills, something my mother would never think about. But Mecca's mom believed it was better to put her daughter on birth control than to have an unwed teenage mother.

Mecca was very sexually active. However, she was always catching infections and diseases. Her mom constantly lectured her about using condoms, but Mecca never listened, saying her friend didn't like using "raincoats".

It seemed like Mecca was always in the clinic being treated for something. One time she caught syphilis, then a month later caught gonorrhea. Despite all of that, she still refused to use condoms.

When I finally told them about Dee, they said they couldn't wait to meet him. I excitedly told my friends that he was the best thing to ever happen to me, and they high-fived me with the same enthusiasm.

It wasn't that I needed their approval or anything; I just wanted to see what they thought. They were like a second family to me, and we were about to have our first "family gathering". I arranged for them to meet Dee at the basketball court the next day. I was so excited that I had trouble sleeping that night.

Mecca and Avalon called me early the next morning because there were thick black clouds in the sky. The wind was blowing hard, and it was a dreary day. We were sad because we knew that if it rained, the brothers wouldn't be playing ball. To make matters worse, the rain poured down for three whole days.

We talked about going to the movies, but pondered how to get there. The only person who could have taken us was Avalon's stepfather. Mecca's mom was a bingo addict, and told us she was going to play bingo that night to win the five-thousand-dollar jackpot. My mom and dad only had one car, and it was for dad to go to work.

Avalon finally got up enough nerve to ask her stepfather to drive us to the cinema. Avalon's father refused, saying she could catch a bus and he would pick us up after he took care of some business. He gave Avalon some money and we were on our way.

We were planning to see "Shaft" and couldn't wait to get there. Though we had bus fare, we didn't use it. It was easier to stick out our thumbs and hitch a ride. We always hitchhiked to get to where we wanted to go.

Our parents warned us of the dangers hitchhiking presented, but we thought we were invincible. We did it anyway, and just didn't tell our parents. We always laughed and said what they didn't know wouldn't hurt them, not realizing how foolish we were.

We would stick out our thumbs, knowing that within seconds four or five cars would stop to give us a lift. It made us feel special, and we always made a show of choosing which car we would get into.

We would only ride in the baddest cars. We had to be impressed by the appearance of the car. And the driver had to be a ten. We refused to ride with ugly dudes, no matter how expensive their car was. We would have rather caught the bus or walked.

That day we chose to ride with a handsome brother that had slicked back hair. He was driving a shiny black van. It was a nice ride and accommodated all of us, so we got in. When he dropped us at the mall, it was about four-thirty.

The minute we got there, we headed to the payphones to call our boyfriends. Freddie told Avalon that he would get one of his partners to drop him there. Mecca didn't want to be bothered with any of her boyfriends, so she decided to chill.

As usual, I couldn't get in touch with Deandre. His Marine friends gave me the same line: "You just missed him." Even though Dee said I could call him anytime, they always said that whenever I called for him.

The theatre was inside the mall, which was always crowded. It was more crowded than usual that day. It seemed like everybody who was anybody was up in there, including a few foes.

We saw some girls from another park who didn't like the idea of Freddie and Avalon going together. They used to beat up Avalon at school for messing with Freddie, but it never deterred her from seeing him.

As Avalon and Freddie walked past them at the mall, the girls rolled their eyes at Avalon and called her a slut. Avalon didn't pay them any mind, as usual. She just kept hugging on Freddie and kissing him.

The movie wasn't going to start until six, so Mecca and I separated from Avalon and Freddie. We knew that they wanted to be alone for a while. Mecca and I went into some of the clothing stores to browse before the movie started.

We checked out the hottest and latest fashions, cooing over a sexy pair of hip-huggers on the rack. We also tried on some tight sizzler dresses that came with matching panties. We made a mental list of things we wanted, and

I told Mecca I was going to do some serious shopping when I got my babysitting money.

We walked over to the lingerie section, where I checked out some revealing lacy underwear that was lavender in color. It even had a matching brassiere. Since I looked good in pastels, I took them to the cashier.

While I was paying, I told Mecca that I was going to bring Dee up there so he could buy me some of this stuff for my birthday. She was shocked to find out that Dee bought me clothes and jewelry. I was more shocked when she told me her boyfriends didn't.

I guess Mecca got tired of not having, because she started shoplifting. She would carry large purses so she could stuff a lot of merchandise. When we had left the store, Mecca had taken two sizzler dresses, two pairs of hip-huggers, three halter tops, four tub tops, and a backless blouse. Even though she knew it was wrong to steal, she saw it as the only way to get new clothes.

The movie was about to begin, and we couldn't wait to drool over Richard Roundtree. But our first stop before entering the theatre was the concession stand. While we were loading up on snacks and popcorn, Mecca and I noticed some dudes checking us out.

They came over to where we were standing and introduced themselves. One of them was tall and light-skinned, with a gigantic Afro. He said his name was Kyle, and that he was a musician.

His partner was dark-skinned, with a mole on his right cheek. He was definitely fine. He told me his name was Darnell. He was an artist and wore his hair long and slicked back, making his handsome features stand out more.

They started asking us the usual questions: where we lived, our names, our signs, then tried to get our phone numbers. I was a little hesitant about giving my number out because of Dee. I was in love with him, and other men were non-existent to me.

However, I did get tired of being alone when my friends went out with their boyfriends. I was tired of "just missing him" when I called. Tired of not seeing him when I wanted to see him. Tired of not seeing him during the holidays because he had to "got to another base for guard duty".

I decided that Darnell could satisfy some of my loneliness, so I gave him my number. Mecca made it known that she was interested in Kyle, immediately giving him her phone number. With flirty eyes she told him not to wait too long to call.

There was so much noise in the movie theatre. The previews kept rolling, but everyone was impatient for the movie to start. The whole theatre was yelling and making noise, but finally the movie began.

I immediately grew hypnotized by Shaft in his black leather pants and matching trench coat. The brother sitting next to me remarked that he had the exact same outfit, and I smirked in response. I knew one thing: if Dee wore that outfit, everyone in the theatre would have been checking him out.

Once the movie ended, the dudes that we met earlier walked us to the lobby. They asked us if we needed a ride home, but we declined, saying our ride was coming. As they were saying good-bye, Mecca reminded Kyle to call her that night.

We saw Avalon and Freddie standing against the wall kissing good-bye. After giving Freddie a long kiss, she drifted over to us, still caught up in her love-filled haze.

In a dream-like voice, she whispered, "I had a really good time."

Avalon's stepfather was sitting in his car smoking a cigarette. It was impossible to miss that gigantic brown and yellow station wagon in the parking lot. He had the radio cranked way up, and we could hear the disc jockey all the way across the parking lot.

Her stepfather didn't utter a word the entire ride home. Instead, he smoked one cigarette after another. The radio DJ Soul Ranger played one of my favorite songs, "Tears of a Clown". It seemed like Smokey Robinson knew exactly what I was going through.

Avalon's stepfather dropped off Mecca first, then me. He never responded to us, even when we both said thanks and good night. I barely had enough time to tell Avalon that I'd see her tomorrow before he sped off.

CHAPTER SIX

I went into my room and hung up my green pleather coat. My parents couldn't afford real leather, but mine passed for the real thing pretty well. Afterwards, I went into the kitchen to see what mom had cooked.

Before looking in the pot, I sneakily looked around to make sure no one was around. I didn't wash my hands, and if my mom knew I was digging through her food with dirty hands, she would have beaten me until I was black and blue.

I thought about Dee as I munched on some chitterlings, collard greens, cornbread and black-eyed peas. After consuming a few helpings, I finished the meal with a large piece of watermelon. I smiled softly, thinking it was sweet and delicious, just like Dee.

I retired to my bedroom. Before my head could hit the pillow, I heard a loud rap on my door, then my father's booming voice.

"Some boy called this evening, Tunisia," he yelled. "I don't mind you gettin' phone calls, but you betta not be courtin', or you'll be sorry. I'm tired of you comin' in this house later and later, too… gon' be puttin' a stop to that."

I rolled my eyes as he continued, "And your momma told me that you been unruly while I was out to sea. You betta put yourself in check, young lady!"

My dad slipped the phone message under my door. I smiled when I saw it was from Dee. He was hardly a boy. And it was good thing my mother and father didn't know. They could never know.

I never introduced Dee to my parents. How could I? He was much older than I was, and I knew my mom and dad wouldn't approve. Plus, if they found out I was courting, they would have beaten me to death probably.

I kept Dee as far away from my house as possible. I had no intention of ever letting Dee meet any of them. My parents wouldn't understand, and would ask way too many questions. Not to mention, Dee would find out that I was only fifteen.

At about eleven-thirty that evening, Mecca called to tell me that Kyle was coming to the park to see her. She asked if I would come along, and I said cool. We agreed to meet at the basketball court at six the next evening.

I was standing by the court waiting for Dee when Avalon and Freddie arrived. She was excited to finally meet Dee, but remained patient. I told them to wait while I went inside to get a bag of chips.

As I walked around the corner, I noticed people playing bingo in one room and shooting craps in another. I approached the vending machine and dropped my quarter in. Just then, I felt an arm wrap around my waist.

I quickly turned to face my assailant, then smiled widely when I saw that it was Dee. He wore a matching grin on his face. He asked me where I was when he called, and I nonchalantly replied that I was at the movie with my friends.

He kept badgering me with questions, as if he didn't believe me. It was weird for him to act like he didn't trust me. I told him that I called the barracks to see if he could meet me up there, and he replied that he never got the message.

I let it go, telling him that I wanted him to meet my partners. He said cool and followed me outside. Suddenly, he stopped and told me that he needed to go tell his friends that he wasn't going to ball with them that day.

I held back a sigh of impatience and asked him what happened. He said that he hurt his leg at work and wouldn't be able to play on it. Then he asked if I would go for a ride with him, like he was trying to change the subject. I told him I'd go, but only after he met my friends. He seemed agitated about it but finally agreed.

Mecca came around the corner wearing red hot pants. All the brothers were checking her out, and she smiled widely, knowing she was too hot. She sashayed harder as the guys whistled and made suggestive remarks at her. But her eyes lit up when she heard a familiar voice. It was Kyle, who pulled up in a shiny gray Riviera.

After Kyle and Mecca exchanged small talk, they walked over to me and Dee. Then I called Avalon and Freddie over, who arrived hand in hand. We all introduced ourselves, then I told my friends that I was going somewhere with Dee. We said our goodbyes then went our separate ways.

Dee started kissing and caressing my neck, and I thought about how good it felt to be in his arms again. I let his tongue absorb my mouth, and his hands moved wherever they wanted to go. We finally walked back to his Mustang and got in. I waved bye to my friends, who winked back and waved.

CHAPTER SEVEN

Dee pressed his foot on the accelerator, and within seconds we were pushing seventy on the interstate. I told him to slow down, but he refused. He loved going fast, and thought life in the fast lane was more exciting.

Thankfully, he finally slowed down. He asked me to open his glove compartment and fire up a joint for us. I opened it and a small gold case fell out. When I opened the case, there were at least twenty joints inside.

I lit one and took five or six puffs. I had never smelled marijuana like that and screwed up my face with confusion. It was strong stuff! Within seconds I was unable to talk or think clearly. There was also a strange sensation in my stomach.

I began to feel out of control and started to get paranoid. I asked him what the hell were we smoking, and he replied that it was called "wacky weed". He said to just relax and let it do its thing, pulling out a bottle of Wild Irish Rose from the cooler. We drank from the same cup as I tried to chill but couldn't.

I began to feel very uncomfortable because it was getting so late. I asked Dee to take me home, but he wouldn't. He said he just wanted to spend some time with me. He complained that he lied to his friends about hurting his leg so he could use it as an excuse not to play ball.

I was half listening, knowing that when I got home, I would probably be grounded. As I fretted, Dee kept driving until we reached the beach. We got out of the car and began to walk hand in hand on the beach.

The evening was nice and warm, and the moon was big and bright. It looked so close, it felt like I could reach out and touch it. Even though the night was romantic and seemingly perfect, I wasn't having a good time. I kept telling Dee that I had to be home early, but he didn't want to hear it.

Instead, he kept feeling me up, refusing to listen to what I said. I was so angry! All Dee thought about was sex. It seemed like when he wanted my body, he blocked out anything else about me.

We continued walking along the shoreline, the waves splashing on our feet and legs. It was really late at that point. The only people on the beach were lovers, and it was clear why Dee brought me here.

He found an isolated area under some trees and immediately started touching my body. However, I was not in the mood. I kept pushing his hands away, telling him that I didn't want to do it and that I needed to get home soon.

He didn't care, and kept murmuring about how bad he wanted me, but I still refused to give in to his demands. He didn't care. He took my body anyway, kissing me and telling me how much he needed me and loved me. I felt angry, frustrated, and afraid.

I also felt confused. The term "date rape" never entered my mind, but I wondered if my boyfriend was allowed to do it to me, even if I didn't want to. We were in a relationship that included lots of sex, so was I allowed to say no? I was upset as he moved on top of me, but my 15-year-old self felt very powerless against a 23-year-old Marine.

I looked up at the moon, which was full and mesmerizing. I listened to the ocean waves, allowing their dancing movements on the rocks hypnotize me into a more relaxed state. The pot began to dull my judgment.

"Why fight him?" I thought to myself, closing my eyes. "I love him, he loves me. He just wants to be with me..."

Even though I felt like he should have listened to what I wanted, I let it go as usual. He felt good on top of me, and the combination of alcohol, weed, and his body was too much for me to overcome. I finally gave in to Dee's movements.

I held on to him for dear life, my eyes still closed tightly. He must have been experiencing the same thing as me because he held on just as tight. He gave me one final kiss, and then it was time to go.

He drove me back to our meeting place, talking the entire time about how good life was. He kept saying I was the best thing in his life, and how lucky he felt that he met me.

CHAPTER EIGHT

Mecca, Avalon, and I decided we weren't going to school the next day. Instead, we made plans to go to the Grill to hang out and gossip. Hooking was a regular thing for us, something we did at least once a week.

I never worried about missing my lessons because I always caught up with one of my classmates. I would get the notes and assignments for each class, then study like a maniac. When test time came, I always passed with straight A's. I just had a gift for retaining information.

We caught the bus to the Grill, which was a store across the street from a different high school than ours. That was where the in-crowd went to play cards, eat, dance, and shoot craps. The place was always jamming.

The owner was a laid-back elderly man who could never control the influx of students. As soon as a group of students left, a larger group would enter. So rather than fighting us, he made money off of us instead. We didn't care because back then we failed to see the importance of school. We were learning things on the street that we felt pertained to our real lives.

That day the music was jumping, and everyone was laughing and having a good time. Suddenly, the door burst open and a large group of cops raided the place. Pandemonium immediately broke out, and me and my friends high-tailed it for the exit doors at lightning speed.

We saw that the truant officer and several cops had the Grill surrounded, so we cut through an alley and onto a side street. I was almost too scared to look back, but I did. I caught a glimpse of the owner getting arrested, but I wasn't worried about him. If I got caught, I'd be on restriction for a small eternity.

We didn't stop running until we reached the mall. We stopped at one of the drugstores so Avalon could buy some cigarettes. Mecca and I were standing by the magazine racks when Avalon walked up and whispered that she just stole a pack of cigarettes, a bottle of perfume, and some breath mints.

At that point, we headed for the door.

Avalon knew stealing was wrong, but she didn't care. She had a problem, but we didn't know how to help her. She had only recently picked up her stealing habit, but we never said anything. The thought of me and Mecca getting in trouble if she got caught never crossed our minds.

She was walking down the street coughing and puffing with no sense of guilt. Her clothes had a deep stench of smoke. We told Avalon that if we could smell the smoke on her, we knew her parents would be able to.

Avalon merely reached into her purse and pulled out the bottle of Charlie perfume she had stolen. It was a very expensive brand. She sprayed some on her neck and clothes, then misted some on me and Mecca like it was air freshener.

We rushed home, knowing all we had to do was make it back by the time our school bus got there, then casually walk with the other students that actually got off the bus. Thankfully, we made it to the bus stop on time.

The only problem was that my brother would be on that bus. We attended the same school and he was a model student. He never skipped school and always told on me. He would probably tell my parents that he didn't see me at school all day.

I went into my bedroom and sat on the bed, wondering what the assignments were in English. That was my best subject, since I really enjoyed poetry and grammar. I decided it was time to do a "tattletale check".

I cautiously went into the kitchen to see what my mom was cooking. I had a bit of small talk with her, quickly growing relieved when she didn't say anything about my cutting class. I knew I had it made, since my brother had already left for the basketball court.

I remembered that I had to call my classmate to get the assignments, so I pulled the cord into my room. I got out my notebooks and a pencil then called my classmate, preparing to make a list of what I needed to do.

Once I got all of the assignments, I stared at the long list in shock. That teacher must have been crazy, giving us all that work! He wanted us to read the first five chapters of a boring novel, then critique each chapter. I just couldn't see the benefits of reading the books he selected.

I called Mecca and Avalon to complain about my homework assignment. They cheered me up, and we planned to play hooky from school the next day. We decided to hit up the Strip for entertainment.

In the meantime, Mecca and Kyle were getting along really well. He started teaching Mecca how to drive his Riviera, even though she didn't have a permit. Mecca was so happy that she had Kyle, and spent so much time with him that she stopped seeing her other boyfriends. When you saw Kyle, you saw Mecca. Even Mecca's mom and siblings liked him.

To our surprise, Mecca's mom would let Kyle spend the night. He would play his saxophone for Mecca for hours. Kyle could surely blow on that sax, and Mecca fell deeper for him with each note he played.

She told us that Kyle was the only man she needed. Our friend was finally in love. We were happy and grew closer as friends, spending a lot of time together. Life seemed to be truly good.

Kyle spent a lot of time at Mecca's. Her mom even cooked for Kyle and washed his clothes. Kyle was almost twenty-six years old, but Mecca's mom continued to let Mecca be around him. She also let him continue to hang out around their house.

Kyle had been around. He was a very talented and handsome man. And he was Mecca's man. He made her better. Mecca told us that everything was fine between her and Kyle until Mecca's mom came into play…

CHAPTER NINE

Mecca went through some serious changes. She called me and Avalon sounding really frantic one day, saying that we needed to talk immediately at the rec center. Even though Avalon was going through her own issues, she always was a good listener and offered solutions.

When we got to the center, Mecca was clearly upset. She kept saying that she was going to run away. She was talking really fast and sounded a little crazy. We told her to calm down and explain what happened.

She tearfully blurted out that she caught Kyle in bed with her mother. Our mouths fell open in shock as she said that Kyle wanted to be with her mom now. At first, we couldn't believe it. We thought Mecca was lying, but she wasn't. She took us to her house to show us the proof.

We walked in the living room, then immediately stopped in our tracks. Mecca's mom was all over Kyle. They were lying on the sofa watching television, no signs of remorse on Mecca's mom's face.

It was true. Mecca's mom had taken Kyle from her own daughter. We couldn't believe she could be so insensitive to Mecca's feelings. Sure, she had been without a man for a long time, but that was truly dirty.

What about Mecca's pride and self-esteem? She already had to grow up dealing with taunts from kids over how she dressed. When she finally found a man that made her feel worthy, her mom took that away.

Mecca told us that her mother said Kyle was way over twenty-one and that he needed to be with a woman, not a child. Avalon and I argued back, asking why she didn't say that before Kyle and Mecca became so involved.

At first Mecca's mom accepted the fact that Mecca was going with an older man. Now she was saying he was too mature for her? We knew why her mother had such a change of heart. She wanted Kyle for herself. We argued how unfair that was, cursing her mother's hypocrisy and selfishness. We had our friend's back.

Mecca was going under. She said that everything was fine until her mother stole Kyle from her. She couldn't believe that her own mom would do that to her. Instead of apologizing, her mother repeatedly berated her, sneering that all was fair in love and war.

Mecca simply gave up, admitting defeat in silence. She knew better than to fight. How can a daughter compete with her mother for the intimate affections of the same man? It simply wasn't in Mecca's heart, even though it was in her mom's.

Every time her mother and Kyle kissed or hugged, Mecca said something inside her died. Whenever her mom and Kyle went out, Mecca ached. Every day she thought about how her mother betrayed her. They used to be so close before Kyle entered their lives. Now they were enemies.

Mecca's pain grew daily. It ate away at her very being. She suffered in silence everyday as she watched them flaunt their love right in her face. Whenever she thought about her mother stealing her boyfriend, her chest felt like it was splitting. Every time she thought about Kyle making love to both of them, something inside her ripped.

She wanted revenge. She thought about different ways to kill Kyle while making her mother watch. Then she thought about murdering her mother. She thought about killing them while they were hugged up in bed. Mecca also thought about killing herself.

Sadly, she was desperate. She had finally convinced herself that suicide was the only way out. She said that life was not worth living if she couldn't have Kyle. Despite all the pain he caused her, she was still in love with that dog, even though she hid it from us.

Mecca grew extremely depressed. She confided in us daily because she couldn't deal with it, but we didn't have any answers. This was completely new to us, and we were just young, naïve girls. It was something that happened, and Mecca had to deal with it.

When there were no answers, you figure that it's just a part of life. You either dealt with it and continued moving down life's journey, or you could self-destruct. Though I felt powerless, I also felt bad for Mecca. The same man who brought her so much happiness had brought her even more sadness and pain.

Mecca was drowning in sorrow, and kept thinking of ways to make Kyle and her mother pay for what they did. She kept returning to the thought that if she ended her sorry life, they would never forgive themselves. She no longer had hope for the future; they were all vanquished by her mother and Kyle.

Mecca usually cried herself to sleep, but one night was awakened by their laughter. It was about two in the morning, and Kyle and her mother had just returned from some house party. They were loudly talking about how the party jammed. Mecca quickly jumped out of bed and ran down the hall, spying on Kyle and her mom.

They began to slow dance to a Marvin Gaye song. Kyle held Mecca's mother so tenderly, Mecca had to look away for a moment. He held her mom the exact same way he used to hold Mecca. He started whispering sweet nothings, and Mecca's mom was loving it.

He started nibbling her earlobes, then her neck, as hot tears dripped down Mecca's face. When Kyle gave her mom a deep, passionate kiss, Mecca had to close her eyes. The pain was too much.

When she opened her eyes, she saw her mother caressing Kyle's back and shoulders. He looked into her mother's eyes and told her he loved her. He cradled her chin, kissing her lovingly.

Meanwhile, Mecca died a little more. They kissed. She wept. They caressed. She sobbed. They danced. She died. They whispered. She prayed for the pain to stop.

The music ended and they finally stopped dancing. Kyle told Mecca's mom to put on something sexy while he poured them some wine. Knowing her mother was headed upstairs, Mecca quickly headed back to her room.

She started thinking about how much she hated that low-down, dirty dog Kyle. Then she thought about how much she loved that low-down, dirty dog. There was a thin line between love and hate, and it just snapped for Mecca. She didn't know what to think anymore.

She wanted him back. She wanted him dead. She wanted to kiss him again. She wanted to kick him repeatedly. She wanted him to be gone forever, while wanting him to be her man again.

Mecca heard her mom scurrying to her room to don her sexy nightgown. She would probably put on the red one with black lace. It was sheer, sexy, and elegant, unlike the mismatch panties and brassieres Mecca was forced to steal and wear.

Her mom would probably put on those black fish nets with the garters. She knew how to entice a man. She knew how to be a woman. Mecca heard glasses chime together and knew Kyle was in her mother's bedroom with her. The moment was punctuated by the sound of her mom's bedroom door thundering shut.

Mecca went back to her room and quietly closed the door, shedding tears of pain and shame. She was ashamed of her mother for doing such a thing, but also ashamed of herself for letting it happen. She wondered if there was anything she could have done to prevent it. She was just ashamed of the whole damned incident.

How could she go on facing her friends, her neighbors, and even Kyle and her mother? How could she live, knowing that everybody knew her mom was sleeping with her daughter's ex-boyfriend?

Mecca felt like she couldn't take it anymore. Everything finally reached the boiling point. Each day got worse and worse. Kyle and her mother grew even more disrespectful with how they flaunted their love everywhere.

Mecca kept comparing herself to her mother, her self-esteem falling lower and lower. Her mom was very attractive, without having to wear any makeup. Her skin features were glamorously reminiscent of Donna Summers.

Mecca's mother never had to use any moisturizers or masks to retain her beauty. She had big, pretty legs like Tina Turner, and wore stylish, up-to-date clothing. Nothing like the old-fashioned clothes that Mecca was used to sporting.

Since Mecca's mom was closer to Kyle's age than Mecca, the two of them related to each other better. Their conversations were very intelligent and in-depth, with the two of them discussing world issues for hours at a time. Mecca's mom was a great conversationalist.

She was also extremely charming. She kept up with the latest trends, community issues, political updates, and was very well-spoken. Whenever Kyle tried to have those conversations with Mecca, it was usually him doing most of the talking while she listened intently. Mecca resolved that she couldn't compare to her mom when it came to Kyle.

CHAPTER TEN

We all finally reached our sixteenth birthdays. I still babysat for Leslie regularly, and I loved every minute of it. Her children were half-black and white. We called them mulattos, and they were as cute as the day is long, with pretty curly 'Fros and dark features.

As for Leslie, she looked okay for a white girl. I didn't think she was a day over nineteen, though. She had blonde hair that she wore in an Afro. Leslie was well proportioned, and swore she was black. She had a big butt like South Carolina girls and coke-bottle hips. She always joked that life played a trick on her, and that she was supposed to be black, not white.

I was bathing them when Leslie came home unexpectedly. She had a fine man with a dark complexion with her. When I looked up, she told him to go into the back room. With a tiny smile, she asked if I would take the children to the park for an hour.

I nodded and quickly got the children dressed and in their strollers. As we were leaving, two more men entered the house. I pushed the kids around the park for over an hour, wondering when it would be okay for me to go back.

When I returned, one of the men was still there. I could hear him arguing with Leslie about something. Leslie screamed that she wanted her money, but he told her that he wasn't going to give her a dime.

I walked in and saw her grabbing for his wallet. The man roughly slapped her across the face several times, and she started fighting him back. Pretty soon they were rumbling like cats and dogs. I was standing there in disbelief, watching him repeatedly punch her in the face.

Leslie finally noticed me standing there and ordered me to take the kids into the back room. I asked her if she wanted me to call the police, hurriedly pushing the stroller to the back room.

She breathlessly replied, "No, please. Whatever you do, don't call them."

By this time, her nose and mouth were bleeding profusely. A thick pool of blood covered the upper part of her white blouse, and her eyes were black and blue. It looked like she couldn't take much more of a beating.

Just then, he picked her up and threw her across the room. She landed on her beautiful glass living room table, shattering it to a million pieces. I thought she was out for the count, but she quickly got up, snatching a lamp from a nearby table and smashing him over the head with it.

His head began to bleed, his blood spurting out in many different directions. As it splashed the walls and floor, I started screaming. I yelled that I was going to call the cops if he didn't leave.

At first, he started for the door, then he suddenly turned around and socked Leslie in the stomach. She dropped to the floor like a sack of potatoes. Instead of walking out, he kicked her several times. Finally, he walked out, a trail of blood following him to his Camaro.

I ran over to Leslie, who was still on the floor surrounded by a puddle of blood. He really messed her up. She was still bleeding from her mouth and nose, but I could see one of her teeth had been knocked out as well.

Every time I tried to help her up, she would haplessly fall back down. I was so worried, since she was barely conscious. I kept asking Leslie if she wanted me to call an ambulance, but she declined.

"Just try to help me up so I can clean myself up," she muttered weakly, struggling to her feet.

I helped her to the bathroom, letting her put her full weight on me the entire time. When she saw herself in the mirror, her body began to shake and she just cried. I ran some bath water for her and let her soak for an hour.

I treated her wounds as best I could, but I didn't really know what to do. She had deep cuts and bruises all over her body, and I wondered if some glass was still embedded in her. She really should have gotten some medical attention.

Because it was the weekend, I called my parents to see if it was all right to stay with Leslie and the kids. My mom immediately said yes, since she liked knowing where I was. I didn't tell my mom about what happened to Leslie. If they knew about the fight, they'd never let me babysit for her again. The how would I be able to see Dee at night?

I actually owed Leslie. The night Dee took me to the beach and had me out super late, Leslie covered for me. She told my parents that I had been babysitting for her, and apologized for any mix-ups.

My parents bought it because I was always at Leslie's house babysitting anyway. They liked that I earned my own money and was doing something responsible. But if Leslie hadn't lied for me that night, I would have been on punishment for two months.

At first, I didn't know that Leslie was emotionally and physically hurting, but as time went on, I started to take care of her right along with the kids.

She opened up to me about her personal life, which was lonely, exciting, and dangerous.

Leslie told me that she was a "lady of the night", and that was how she made her money. She said it was hard for her to make it on the food stamps and welfare alone, so she had to supplement her income.

She also admitted that she had two other children that lived with her aunt. Apparently, that aunt was the only one in the family that hadn't disowned her. Her other family members did not like the men she chose. They considered her "white trash" because she dated black men.

Two weeks later, Leslie was up to her "tricks" again. It wasn't unusual for ten to twelve dudes to visit her in one day. Leslie was making a lot of money. At first when I didn't know her occupation, she would tell me to take the kids to the park.

Since she had confided in me, Leslie felt comfortable enough to say, "I'll be in the back room working, doing my thing. Keep the kids busy in the living room."

Leslie paid me a lot of money during that time because I had helped her so much. I was itching to go shopping. That money was burning a hole in my pockets, and I needed to hit downtown.

I called my partners to see if they could go. Avalon said she was grounded for "a while" because her parents found cigarettes in her purse. Mecca told me she was just going to chill all day. That left me on my own.

I needed a new outfit because Dee planned to take me to see "Shaft" the next week. I didn't mind that I was seeing it again, as long as I was with him. I would watch any movie a hundred times just to be with that man.

CHAPTER ELEVEN

I started to head downtown to do my shopping, but changed my mind at the last minute. Instead, I decided to hit the Exchange on the base. I had a lot to pick up, and it would be cheaper to shop there. My brothers wanted me to buy them some comic books, while my sisters wanted Barbie dolls.

I walked to the entrance of the base and boarded the shuttle bus to the piers. While on the bus, I happened to look out and saw a car that looked just like Dee's. I couldn't tell if the driver was Dee, though.

As the car passed by, I did see a woman's face on the passenger's side. She was a very pretty lady with a mole on her right cheek. She had a short Afro, high cheekbones, and was sporting long, metallic earrings.

I couldn't say for sure if that car was Dee's. I tried to catch the license plate before the car passed, but I couldn't make out the numbers in time. I decided to check it out later when I had some time.

The bus let me off right outside the Exchange, where a rush of excitement immediately filled me. Second only to Dee, shopping was the love of my life. I could do it all day, every day, and I felt complete every time I bought something new.

I headed straight to the "Misses" department and browsed the name brand clothing. They sure were expensive. If I hadn't been baby-sitting so much, I wouldn't have been able to afford any of it. My mom and dad definitely couldn't afford those threads.

I noticed a bad pair of hip huggers, along with a halter top that went well with it. My eyes narrowed and my shopping lust was officially ignited! I found a blazer to go with the outfit, then headed over to the shoe department, ignoring the jewelry section. The only jewelry I was interested in was a ring on my finger.

There were a lot of people out shopping that day because it was the thirtieth, military payday. I saw a few Marines shopping in the clothing department, while others were standing at the jewelry counter browsing necklaces. We all had one thing in common: we loved shopping!

My last stop was the hair section, because no matter how good you look in your clothes, if your hair wasn't right then nothing was. I stocked up on Afro Sheen products, ignoring the makeup. I already had some at home, even though I was forbidden to wear it. I hid it between my mattresses so my nosy sisters didn't find it.

I headed over to the health and beauty section for some feminine products, then finally swooped around to pick up some comic books and Barbies. I decided to surprise Dee with a Parliament Funkadelic record as well. He told me he always wanted it but never had the time to buy it.

I was so busy shopping and feeling like a grown up that I almost missed the bus. I stumbled on with all of my bags, thinking about how nice it was to have my own money to buy things. I felt blessed knowing I didn't have to steal, and thanked God that I had a good job that paid me well.

By the time I got home, it was almost time for Dee to pick me up from the rec center. I was getting ready when the phone rang. I was surprised to hear it was Darnell, the guy I met at the Shaft movie. It was good hearing his voice for a change.

He told me that his studio was doing well, and asked if he could paint a portrait of me. Flattered, I immediately told him yes. Darnell laughed, then said he was just waiting for me to set the date and time. We decided next Friday at six would be perfect.

Darnell gave me directions to his studio, telling me he was excited to meet me there. I was just as enthusiastic, and not just about the portrait. I was in love with Dee, but talking to Darnell gave me a different kind of feeling. I asked him to call me later because I had more questions.

I rushed to the rec center, knowing Dee was already there waiting for me. I was rushing so much that I almost forgot to put on my makeup and spray Afro Sheen on my hair. I hadn't seen or heard from him in a few days, and was really missing him.

He was sitting on the hood of his car when I walked up. He excitedly jumped off the hood and embraced me, saying I looked good enough to eat. I questioned him about where he'd been for the past few days, and he shrugged me off, saying he was on assignment unexpectedly at another base.

I let it go, instead deciding to enjoy being with my man. I thought we were going to the movies, but to my surprise, Dee had something else in mind. His words were like music to my ears when he said, "Baby, I have something special in store for you."

I was excited as we got on the interstate and started driving across the Chesapeake Bay Bridge, where we could see the fearless ships and destroyers on the base. I always loved seeing the fleets and their display of strength.

There was an aircraft carrier crossing the bay with several jets on deck. It was such an amazing ship! It pushed its way through blue-gray water that resembled blankets of steel under the setting sun. The waves slapped the sides of the ships with furious force, keeping my gaze transfixed we crossed the bridge.

I always enjoyed travelling through the underwater tunnel. I was so used to driving through it that I didn't know it was a world-famous channel. When we finally reached the entrance of the tube, Dee tensed up. He was claustrophobic and hated going through the tunnel.

However, Dee said he was giving me a treat for being so sweet. He was obviously bothered by being in the tunnel, but he kept on driving, nervously repeating that he was doing it because he had a surprise for me on the other side.

He began to sweat and fidget in his seat, and I grabbed his hand comfortingly. A few minutes later, we were out of the tunnel and Dee was back to his normal self. I giggled a little at his boyish bravery, but it made me love him that much more.

Minutes later, he pulled into the parking lot of a fancy restaurant. I started wishing I had dressed properly for the occasion. It was like he could read my mind, because Dee immediately said that he liked me just the way I was, commenting that I looked good in my hip-huggers.

The atmosphere and décor of the restaurant was fabulous. We ate venison, sea soufflé, and cheesecake off of fine china and crystal. After our meal, we drank a glass of white wine. The setting was so romantic that I hoped the night would never end.

We talked about so many things. It was like I had known Dee for many years. I thanked him repeatedly for what was clearly an expensive dinner. Dee tipped the waiter and paid the bill while I went to the restroom.

Dee waited patiently for me by the entrance, and we held hands as we walked out the door. When we got in his car, he asked if I enjoyed myself. I told Dee that it couldn't get any better than that.

"Oh, yes it can," he grinned widely, winking at me.

He pulled out a diamond ring and slipped it on my left ring finger. I couldn't believe it, but there it was. The one piece of jewelry I had always been hoping for. I was in shock that he actually gave me a ring, because we'd only known each other for less than a year.

At that point, I wanted him to know that I had a gift for him, too. I pulled out the album he'd always wanted and handed it to him with a wide smile. He was ecstatic when he saw what it was, and immediately gave me a big kiss.

Finally, we pulled out of the parking lot and got on the freeway. As usual, he pressed the accelerator to the floor. It seemed like only a few minutes had passed before we pulled into the rec center. He gave me a long, passionate kiss and was on his way, leaving me standing alone in the parking lot.

I reached inside my purse for my cold cream and a tissue, wiping off my makeup as I walked home. Everyone was asleep when I got home. I quietly crept to my room, anxious to reminisce about the perfect evening.

I threw myself on the bed and pulled out my diary, then quickly made the latest entry. With the memory of the evening safeguarded on the pages, I locked my diary and returned it to its hiding place. I closed my eyes and imagined I was with Dee as I drifted off to sleep.

CHAPTER TWELVE

Avalon was becoming more and more distant from us. She was still going with Freddie, but we didn't see them together as much anymore. Rumors were flying that Avalon was on hard drugs, but Mecca and I refused to believe them.

It was rough in the 'hood. You could literally smell the stench of poverty in the air. Most of the people in our neighborhood were on welfare, and it was all for various reasons. Poverty knew no color. It's a shame that while we were sending people to the moon, we were powerless to stop hunger, poverty, and homelessness.

Growing up, we mistakenly admired the drug pushers, pimps, prostitutes, and loan sharks. We thought they were the real survivors because they were making big money and had extravagant things.

Our teen years were really hard, mainly because we didn't feel good about ourselves at all. Our self-esteem was low. We were poor and black, and the system never let us forget that. Our parents were so busy worrying about bills and problems in the community that they never had time to sit down and talk to us.

We were having serious adjustment problems. We didn't have any good role models to follow. We needed to be recognized and praised for our endeavors and abilities. We wanted to be surrounded by positive influences that gave us hope.

A lot of teens were very rebellious, vandalizing cars and property. Many started stealing, raping, killing, and doing all kinds of crazy things, seemingly without guilt or shame. Most of the kids in my neighborhood were already in trouble with the law.

The lack of jobs, good educations, and role models didn't help. The racism we experienced, misguided love, and our lack of communication with parents just added fuel to the fire. The overall sense of hopelessness intensified our problems.

Some of the adults in the 'hood had already given up. They became drug addicts, alcoholics, and bums to escape the pressures of the world. Every time they tried to get back on their feet, life would push them back down.

Thank God for the ones who never gave up. The ones who knew the importance of education, and that knowledge was power. Knowing the importance of the educational system, they prospered in spite of the barriers and problems.

Those adults understood the importance of saving and investing, rather than spending all of their hard-earned money. They also knew how vital it was to our community for unity to thrive. They helped their fellow man, opening up legitimate businesses and offering services to our community.

I can honestly say that I respect and appreciate those who were able to overcome all of the negative factors in our everyday lives. The ones who took lemons and made sweet lemonade. Those were our positive role models.

CHAPTER THIRTEEN

Unfortunately, there were more of us who were overcome by the negativity than those who conquered it. Sadly, Avalon fell into that group. We became even more concerned about her when she stopped hanging out with us. She was playing hooky from school more frequently, but not with us.

Every time we asked Freddie about her, he would just say that she hadn't been feeling well lately. Whenever we called her house, her brothers and sisters would say she wasn't accepting phone calls.

We'd heard through the grapevine that Avalon was hanging out at the Grill on a regular basis. Mecca and I decided to play hooky one day to investigate. We prayed that we would find out the rumors about Avalon were false.

There she was, hanging out with a group of local junkies that never went to school. Mecca and I glared at Jughead, Lil' T, Sweet Pea, Joker, and J.J., and wondered what the hell they got our friend into. We couldn't believe Avalon had slipped into the drug subculture. Yeah, we smoked herb and did a line every now and then, but Avalon was going under.

The group she was hanging with always walked around looking dirty and smelling funky. I wanted to cry when I saw Avalon in the same condition. I kept asking myself what could have happened to her to cause such a downfall. Why such a drastic change in appearance, behavior, and friends? What made her stop caring?

She didn't even notice Mecca and I standing there. We watched her leave the Grill with her crusty friends. She casually jumped into the backseat of Jughead's car as if she'd been doing it for years. This was definitely not the Avalon we used to know. She seemed unhappy, tired, jittery, and nervous.

Mecca and I confronted Freddie, forcing him to tell us what was going on. We asked if anything had changed between them. Freddie kept saying no, but we could tell he was lying. We kept badgering him with questions until he finally told us the truth. Avalon was strung out on heroin.

We always had our suspicions that Avalon was dabbling into harder drugs, but we never wanted to believe it. Freddie officially confirmed it that day, and we knew we had to do something.

Freddie said he had been trying to get Avalon to seek help, but she refused to get any. That explained why she was so small and frail. Avalon was naturally petite, but now she looked like a bag of bones.

We decided to try and get Avalon some help. We called the Tranquility Lodge to get some information on rehab. The counselor said the center was built to help people get off of alcohol and drugs.

However, the counselor said it would have to be Avalon's decision. If she agreed, we could send her to the rehab center. He also said not to expect Avalon to go to treatment willingly, and to expect a lot of anger and resistance.

He was exactly right. When we approached Avalon about help, she became enraged and refused to seek help. She viciously cursed out me, Freddie, and Mecca, telling us to mind our own business. She kept saying she didn't have a drug problem, and that we didn't know what we were talking about.

We didn't believe her, though. Because the entire time she was ranting and raving, Avalon the chronic liar, who normally could look you in the eye and lie without flinching, couldn't even look us in the face.

CHAPTER FOURTEEN

Normally, I hated hanging out clothes. But with all the things going on in my life, that day it was like therapy for my troubled mind. I had so many unanswered questions: Why were all these things happening to the people I loved? Did God even care? Especially since it seemed like we didn't deserve such suffering.

My thoughts were interrupted when my mother yelled for me to get the phone. I ran inside to see who it was. I wondered if it would be Dee and if he would do something special to cheer me up. Surprisingly, it was Avalon.

"Tunisia, can you come over?" she asked quietly. "I gotta rap to you."

I told her I'd be over there as soon as I was done hanging out the clothes. There were several loads in the washing machine, which always took a long time to complete because the spin cycle was broken. We always had to wring the excess water out by hand.

We had to finish all of our chores before leaving the house, but they always took longer because nothing ever worked. We had to sweep the carpet because the vacuum cleaner was always broken. But I finally got my part of the chores done.

I rushed off to Avalon's house, which was two blocks away. I wondered what kind of mood Avalon would be in. She had such drastic mood swings since she got hooked on heroin. One day she'd be happy as a lark, the next day she would be angry or depressed.

It seemed like Avalon was nauseated or complaining about some illness lately. I still couldn't believe one of my best friends was using heroin. But it was a painful truth we had to deal with. It didn't matter where you lived or what race you were. Drugs didn't discriminate.

Most of the users were into acid, herb, or cocaine. When heroin came on the scene, teenagers started experimenting and enjoying this new, seemingly exotic drug. But heroin was the most dangerous of them all, and it was consuming our friend.

When I arrived at Avalon's house, she was fully dressed. When I asked her what was going on, she said that Freddie had convinced her to get help. Freddie loyally stuck by her through it all, and talked to one of the counselors on her behalf last week.

They told Freddie it would be best to bring Avalon in on a weekday because the entire staff would be there, but they'd make an exception and see her on Saturday. The counselor wanted to talk to Avalon and see how bad her drug problem was, and ask her how serious she was about breaking her habit.

Avalon told me that she was tired of the drugs and the sickness that came with using them. Avalon asked me if I would go to the facility with her. Wrapping my arms tightly around her, I told her there was no doubt.

Freddie arranged transportation for us to the Tranquility Haven Lodge, and soon we were on the road to get our friend back. We kept encouraging Avalon, telling her how we admired her strength and determination. She had taken a big step by realizing she had a problem. Now she was taking the proper measures to beat it.

We were greeted by a friendly receptionist that asked us to be seated. Minutes later, Ms. Davies, the counselor, came out and led us to her office. Avalon was clearly nervous. Her hands were shaking and beads of sweat were forming on her forehead. When I took her hand for support, her palm was cold and sweaty.

I told Avalon that everything would be cool and to try to relax. We looked around the office, noticing how it was decorated to induce a calming effect. There were many beautiful plants such as ferns, begonias, and roses populating the room.

Her light green drapes matched the walls and carpet, and the pastels were soothing. She also had several pictures of children on her desks, probably her grandchildren. Along the wall was a long, black vinyl couch.

I sat on a green swivel rocker while Avalon sat on the sofa. Ms. Davies told Avalon to relax, that everyone was only there to help. She told Avalon that she was going to ask her a series of questions, and to answer them the best she knew how.

"How long have you been using heroin, Avalon?"

Avalon fidgeted and looked at the floor, then whispered, "About eight months."

I reminded myself to stay cool, even though my jaw wanted to drop. Mecca and I had no clue she had been using hard drugs for that long. That meant she started using around the time Dee and I started dating.

"How much money would you say you spend on drugs, Avalon?" Ms. Davies asked in a concerned tone.

With tears welling in her eyes, Avalon admitted, "About two-hundred a week. I know it sounds bad... but I'm serious about gettin' off this stuff. I just need some help."

"And we'll be providing that help," Ms. Davies assured her. "And you'll have a strong support system around you. Your friends, your parents..."

"No!" Avalon protested, her eyes growing wide. "Please don't tell them!"

Avalon started freaking out in the office when the counselor told her they had to notify her parents. I'd never seen her so scared. Avalon pleaded with Ms. Davies to keep it confidential, but the counselor eventually convinced her that it was in her best interests for her parents to know.

"Besides," Ms. Davies said, gently taking her hand, "we are legally obligated to inform them because you are a minor. But that's not a bad thing. The more people you have around supporting you, the better your recovery will be."

Avalon called me two days later to tell me that Ms. Davies had spoken to her parents. They were all going to start rehab next week. Avalon said her mom was very upset about her addiction, and told Avalon she should have talked to her about any problems.

That was the problem, though. It seemed as though nobody wanted to listen to our problems. Not our parents, the teachers, no one. It felt like adults didn't even care about what we thought or felt.

Even though Mecca was going through her own issues at home, she was still concerned about Avalon. Mecca kept telling me that there had to be an underlying problem with Avalon to make her change her life so drastically.

What was Avalon trying to escape from? Was life that miserable for her? What did she witness that made her a junkie? We asked her several times, but never got a straight answer. She would just accuse us of being in her business, and we would argue back that we were concerned.

Avalon would usually say something flippant like, "Y'all need to attend a four-year college to take up business. Two years to mind your own and two years to leave mine alone."

The start date for rehab came fast for Avalon. She and her parents headed up to Tranquility Haven to make preparations. They still acted like they were in shock about it all, which surprised me. All of the signs were there, so how could they not know Avalon was hooked on drugs?

Ms. Davies didn't judge, though. She was just concerned about getting the best help for Avalon as possible. She asked Avalon's parents if they wanted the in-patient or out-patient treatment. Though Avalon would have preferred in-patient, her parents chose out-patient treatment because it was cheaper.

Avalon started immediately, and was already having a hard time fighting the addiction. Poor Avalon. Whenever she felt at her lowest, Ms. Davies would tell her that with time and proper medication, Avalon wouldn't need heroin anymore.

During her rehab, Avalon finally opened up to us about her darkest moments. She told me that she would sell her body to get drugs, and even articles that belonged to her family members.

She said when that wasn't enough, J.J., Jughead and them would come up with scams to get money. They were all like a family in that way. They leaned on each other for support, love, and mostly drugs.

Time passed quickly, and Avalon was recovering beautifully. Tranquility Haven helped her kick the habit, but most importantly, Avalon helped herself get off the drugs. Avalon was the one who finally said no to drugs.

She started putting on weight again and taking care of her appearance. She dressed nice and did her hair again. Her true skin tone was coming back. Avalon didn't need the syringes. She didn't need the pipes. She didn't need the heroin. Avalon started living again.

Everything was going well except for one thing: she was constantly getting sick. Every time we turned around, Avalon had a cold or something. Despite her health issues, Avalon dove back into her education, and started going back to school without skipping.

She stopped hanging around Jughead and the gang and concentrated on her studies, saying she wanted to be somebody. She told us that she had reached rock bottom and never wanted to go there again. She wanted her education more than ever now, and constantly said that she wanted to be a winner, not a loser.

After church one day, Avalon told me that she wanted to rap to me about something. Her entire family had gone to a friend's house for dinner and she finally felt comfortable talking. When she asked me to come over, I told her I'd be there as soon as I changed my clothes.

When I got home, I could hear the sounds of Kool and the Gang's "Jungle Boogie" blasting through the house. My sisters were in the kitchen helping mom set the table. I yelled for them to not set a place for me.

Right when I finished dressing, my dad called my mom back into their room and they started arguing about something stupid. Every time my dad drank, he would start fussing with my mom over nothing. I had to get out of there!

As I was walking to Avalon's, I saw Kyle and all of Mecca's brothers and sisters in Kyle's car. I didn't see Mecca. She was still mad about what he'd done, so she never went anywhere with them.

I finally got to Avalon's and she let me in immediately. I followed her up to her room, where we sat on her canopy bed. Though she shared her room with all of her sisters, it was very pretty. All of the beds were neatly made with pink comforters, and the pillows were covered with ruffled shams. Pink curtains accented the room as well.

Avalon had been off of drugs for just over a month. After getting comfortable, she admitted that she finally wanted to tell me what had been going on. The real deal about what was going on with her family.

I listened patiently as Avalon told me that she was trying to escape from this world, and drugs gave her that. She wanted to think about fantasy and forget reality. She told me that when she was high on heroin, it felt like she could fly away to another world.

"All my pains and troubles disappeared with heroin," she murmured, staring up at the ceiling. "Nothing and no one could touch me. But now the drugs are gone, and the problem is still here. It's not going away, and I get scared that I'll go back to drugs. How do I deal, Tunisia?"

I looked sympathetically at my friend, feeling powerless yet again. I didn't know what to tell her, or any advice to give her that would help her deal. I didn't even know what she was dealing with. What was going on with Avalon that made her feel powerless as well?

CHAPTER FIFTEEN

I was sitting on Avalon's bed waiting for her to spill her guts when the phone rang. When Avalon answered it, her face instantly morphed into one of fear. She told me that Mecca was on the other end crying hysterically.

Apparently, Mecca and her mother had a big fight about Kyle. Mecca pulled a knife on her mom and Kyle, and everything went crazy in the house. Mecca's mom gathered up the kids and Kyle to get them out of the house, then yelled at Mecca that she'd better be gone when they got back.

After they left, Mecca swallowed a large bottle of pills. She called Avalon to tell her good-bye, and to say that we were the best partners she'd ever had. She was calling to say good-bye, but we knew it was her last-ditch effort to get help.

I couldn't believe it. Mecca was trying to commit suicide, and we were her last hope. I guess she just couldn't deal with it anymore. She was reaching out to us, and this time we couldn't allow ourselves to feel powerless. We had to spring into action.

Avalon started yelling into the phone, asking Mecca what kind of pills she had taken. Finally, Avalon hung up the phone and got to her feet, saying we had to move fast. It sounded to her like Mecca had dropped the phone. But because the line was still open on Mecca's end, we couldn't call out to get her help.

Avalon told me to run to the phone booth around the corner to call for help while she ran over to Mecca's. I called 911 and told them to send paramedics to Mecca's, then called my parents for help as well. I told them the situation and asked them to head over to Mecca's.

Once I got there, I saw Avalon outside screaming at the top of her lungs, trying to get Mecca to open the door. Despite numerous tries, we got no response. We started to panic, wondering if we were too late.

We were scared, but frantic. How long ago had she taken the pills? What kind of pills? What if Mecca was already dead? We needed to get inside immediately, and we didn't care how. We just wanted to save our friend.

Avalon ran to one of the bedroom windows to see if it was unlocked. It wasn't. She started looking around for anything that would break the window. She finally located a large rock and hurled it through the living room window.

After knocking the remaining jagged edges from the frame, Avalon asked me to boost her up so she could climb in. I immediately grabbed her waist and hoisted, my adrenaline pushing my strength into overdrive.

I must have pushed her too hard because she flipped forward, then I heard a large thud as Avalon hit the floor. I heard her rattling off a string of curse words as she limped to the door to let me in.

We searched the entire house for Mecca but couldn't find her. We were running out of time. Where was she? We quickly checked her room but didn't see her. We rechecked the other rooms but still no Mecca. We were running around the house like chickens with no heads.

At that point my parents arrived. We told them that Mecca had taken some pills, but we couldn't find her. My parents helped on the search, and we finally found her. She was in the closet of her brothers' room, curled up in a ball. She appeared to be sleeping, but we knew better.

We pulled Mecca from the closet, feeling like the paramedics would never get there. She was barely breathing and was unconscious. Even when we lifted her, it was pure dead weight. We prayed frantically that God would save her.

Finally, we heard the ambulance sirens approach. It took them less than five minutes to get there, but it seemed like an eternity. Once the police and paramedics raced in our direction, my dad rushed out to signal them in.

The paramedics started asking if we knew what kind of pills she took. When we all said no, he asked us to search around the room to find the pill bottle. After faithfully looking, we finally found the bottle under Mecca's bed.

The medics put an oxygen mask over Mecca's face after they got her on the gurney. By then, her skin tone was a different color. The situation was definitely dangerous for Mecca. We could tell when the medics started putting tubes down her throat to pump her stomach.

Meanwhile, they were rushing to load her into the ambulance. Everyone was freaking out, asking if she would be okay. The medics didn't answer. Instead, they slammed the ambulance doors shut and sped off, sirens screaming.

The police stayed behind to question us for more information. They asked us for the name of Mecca's parents and how they could be reached. The officers said they needed the parents immediately because Mecca's condition didn't look good.

After the police departed, we started praying immediately. We prayed for God to save her. We prayed that Mecca would fight for her life. We begged for God to find a way for some light to pierce her dark world.

It seemed like Mecca had already given up. Even as I prayed for her, I wondered if she would find a reason to fight. Maybe there was one. Otherwise, why did she call us? Maybe at the last moment, she didn't want to die. I wanted to believe that she called us so she could be saved.

True, she was mad at her mother and Kyle. Yes, Mecca's mom unfairly berated her. And despite the fact that Mecca's mom took her man from her and was putting her out, Mecca didn't want to die. At the last moment, Mecca wanted to live in spite of all her problems.

My mom and dad went to the hospital to oversee things. I hoped my dad would act right up there. I could still smell the liquor on his breath. But I still listened to him when he told me to wait at Mecca's so we could tell her mother what happened.

It was public knowledge about Mecca's mom and Kyle. Everyone said Mecca was just a time bomb ready to explode. I was disgusted by the people loitering outside gossiping, though. If everyone knew Mecca was a time bomb, why hadn't any adults stepped in to help her? They found it easier to stand on the sidelines, talking and judging.

Avalon and I sat on Mecca's couch, waiting for her mom to get back. We turned on the TV and were immediately accosted by news stories involving crime, crime, and more crime. Rapes. Murders. Robberies. It never ended.

I got tired of hearing the police sirens and ambulances all the time. I was tired of the poverty, homelessness, and our dysfunctional families. My head was starting to hurt from watching all of the violent imagery, so I told Avalon I was going home for a minute.

I walked home in a deep cloud of thought, wondering about life in general. I couldn't help but worry about Mecca, but I was also concerned about Avalon. She was in the middle of drug recovery. Would the stress of our friend's issues push her back into using?

When I got home, I looked on the stove to find something to eat. I quickly made a plate of barbecue ribs, potato salad, cabbage, a roll and sweet potato pie. After blessing my meal, I called Avalon for an update.

She said that Mecca's family had just pulled up and I needed to come over quick. I wolfed down my food and prepared to leave, while trying to avoid my sisters and brothers. They kept asking the who, what, and where questions. I didn't have time to deal with them; I needed to get to the hospital.

When I arrived at Mecca's house, Avalon had already told her mother and Kyle what had happened. Her mom was freaking out, crying and blaming herself. I was trying not to frown at her, since I felt like she needed to be there for Mecca. At least she still cared, though.

Kyle hugged her and told her that he'd drive everyone to the hospital, but Mecca's mother said no. She decided to drive me and Avalon to the hospital herself. She told Kyle that it would be better if he stayed there and waited. Mecca and I just stared at him in disgust.

When we arrived at the hospital, we found my parents in the emergency waiting area. Mecca's mom asked them how her daughter was doing, and they replied that the doctor hadn't come out yet. So we all sat and waited.

Except for Mecca's mom. She made a mad dash for the emergency room counter to speak to anyone about Mecca's condition. Finally, one of the doctors came out to speak to her about the update.

We didn't know how Mecca was doing, but we kept hoping and remained in prayer. Eventually Mecca's mother brought us bad news: Mecca was in the intensive care unit. Mecca was slow recovering because there was a shortage of oxygen to the brain. She would have to go through a series of tests to find out if any other problems existed.

Thankfully though, the doctors said she would pull through. She would have to remain in the hospital for a while, but they expected her to make a full recovery. It would be a lengthy one, but she would survive that close-call. Thank God.

Since Mecca couldn't have any visitors yet, we decided to leave for the night. Mecca's mom apparently called her father, because we saw Mecca's dad striding in through the main entrance as we left.

My dad dropped Avalon off, then took me and my mother home. When we went into the house, my brothers and sisters ran out of their bedrooms to find out what happened. They listened to my father talk to my mother about what a damn shame it all was.

I must have been too nosy because my mother immediately told me to do the dishes. I didn't mind, though. I was just happy that Mecca pulled through. I was beginning to see that life was a truly precious thing.

CHAPTER SIXTEEN

I was surrounded by women who were struggling with inner demons. I was thankful that I was someone that people felt they could confide in. Whether it was Avalon, Mecca, Leslie… even Venice.

A month after we had our abortions, Venice called me to say that she desperately needed someone to talk to. Her voice grew faint as she rambled about being so depressed because of the abortion.

"Nothing in my life seems important anymore," she continued, her voice trembling. "You know my boyfriend broke up with me when he found out I was pregnant? He gave me three hundred dollars to get it done, then told me never to call him again."

When Venice asked me to come over, I told her I'd be there in an hour. After checking the bus schedule, I decided it would take too long by bus, so I hitched a ride. Even though it was a longer ride, I didn't worry.

Venice lived in an upper-class neighborhood. The houses were modern and large, the lawns beautifully manicured. Everything was expensive, from the houses to the cars parked in the driveways. Venice's house was no exception.

I was greeted by Venice's mother, who directed me to Venice's room. Her tutor was leaving just as I arrived. I was astonished, and wondered just how much a tutor would cost. Did you have to be really sick to get one? I put those thoughts aside as soon as I saw Venice's frail body.

Venice was lounged in a red recliner, a thick white blanket draped around her tiny body. I went over and sat beside her, awestruck by her large bedroom. It was like something out of a beautiful homes and bedrooms magazine.

Her bedroom was spacious and neat, with a stereo system situated in front of a white sofa. Her queen-sized bed had matching sheets, pillows, and a comforter. Her floor model Zenith television sat imposingly next to the entrance of her private bedroom. Venice must have noticed my gawking because she finally spoke.

"I'm glad you could make it, girl," she expressed in a soft voice. Seeing my eyes on her curtains, she added in a brighter tone, "The drapes are from China."

When I still didn't say anything, she asked, "Did your parents drive you?"

She frowned softly when I shook my head, telling her I hitched a ride out there. "It's cool, though," I shrugged. "You seemed really down on the phone."

But to be honest, I was actually thinking to myself, "If I had all of this, I wouldn't have time to be depressed."

"I've been seeing a shrink," she admitted hesitantly. "Too many things happened to me at one time, and I couldn't deal with all of it."

Her voice dropping to a whisper again, she stated, "I won't be coming back to school for a long time."

We talked for hours, and I shared some of the things I had been going through. I felt like if she knew she wasn't alone, maybe she would feel better. I wanted to show her that even though we lived on different side of the tracks, we still had common struggles. But what Venice was about to share would alter my view of life forever.

"Tunisia, I want you to promise that you won't ever tell anyone what I'm about to tell you," she cautiously began.

I promised her that her secret would never go past her bedroom door. After all, I had kept the secret of her abortion, so I told her she could trust me with this secret as well. Venice took a shaky breath and tried to hold back her tears as she spoke.

"One night, I hitchhiked from my friend's house. I had money, but you know how it is: hitching a ride home is always quicker.

"A man in a Chevy picked me up and offered me a ride home. He seemed nice at first, but then he started reaching for me and telling me to take off my clothes. I yelled at him to stop the car and let me out, but he drove faster."

My jaw fell open in shock as Venice continued, "He took me to a secluded area and pulled out a gun. He turned the ignition off and put the gun to my head."

She started to cry into my shoulder, deep sobs racking her body. I put a comforting arm around her and rocked her, trying to console her. Her story was so scary.

"Do you need some water?" I asked gently, stroking her hair.

"No, thank you," she sniffled, wiping her nose with her hand, "I've got to tell somebody about this.

"Anyway, the man kept yelling at me, 'If you don't take those clothes off, I'm gonna blow your brains out!' I was terrified that I would die in that car and my family would never know what happened to me.

"I started nervously pulling off my clothes. I felt like a deer caught in the sight of an unknown hunter. I was crying and praying, then out of habit I recited the twenty-third Psalms. Strangely, he started listening to the words.

"In a voice that was less harsh, he asked, 'What's it gonna be?' I told him I would do anything if he didn't kill me. He raped me in his car then drove me to the nearest bus stop. I cried all the way home."

I didn't know what to say. Just the thought of it... I couldn't even allow myself to visualize the terror Venice must have experienced in that dark car, all alone with a strange man. We always thought we were so invincible when we rode with guys we barely knew. The true dangers never became real until now.

"I've never been able to talk about this to anyone until now," Venice choked out. "That's why I didn't keep that baby. I didn't know if it was my boyfriend's or that rapist's. I just... everything is different now. I wish I could take back that night."

Venice began to cry hysterically, and I kept rocking her in an attempt to soothe her. She cried so hard that I wondered if I should get her mother. But God kept me right there, rocking her back and forth. I didn't know it, but Venice needed that cry. It was healing her soul.

I searched my memory banks for something wise to say, but drew a blank. I was only sixteen and had my own foolish issues. However, God spoke through me in that moment, and I told Venice that her nightmare was over now, like a bridge over troubled waters. I also told her that I wouldn't tell a soul.

It was late and I had to leave, so I told her good-night. She smiled widely at me and gave me a big hug, thanking me for being there for her. I smiled back and left her house with a strange new feeling in my soul.

Once I hit the cool night air, out of habit I stuck my thumb out for a ride. And then, quicker than falling autumn leaves, I dropped my thumb and walked to the nearest bus stop. I'd heard Venice's message tonight. Yes, a beautiful change was taking place in me.

CHAPTER SEVENTEEN

Despite the beautiful changes taking place within me, the 'hood seemed to be immune to the natural changes of life. Day after day we battled for mere existence. Crime was everywhere and relentless. Usually, by the time the cops responded to a call for help, the culprits were eating dessert at McDonalds.

One night while I was baby-sitting for Leslie, there was a loud knock at the door. It was Mo Joe, her estranged husband. Leslie ordered me to never open the door for anyone, so I refused to open it for him as well.

He asked me if she was there and I told him no. He called me a liar and started kicking the door. I yelled that Leslie left over two hours ago, and if he didn't stop kicking the door, I would call the cops.

After a few more kicks, thankfully he finally left. When I told Leslie about it later, she thanked me for not letting him in. Running her hand through her thick blonde hair, she rolled her eyes in annoyance.

"He's no good, and follows me like stink on shit. No matter where I move," she shook her head, "he finds me and breaks in. Whatever he wants, he beats me up and takes it!"

"So why do you deal with that?" I asked in confusion. "Fight back."

"How?" she asked, her blue eyes filling with tears. "The first time he beat me up really bad, I pressed charges against him. But when he got out of jail, he hunted me down and beat me even worse for putting him in jail. I got tired of the double ass-whuppings, so I stopped pressing charges."

Leslie never stayed depressed about Mo Joe for long, though. Brothers were making her rich, and she had no complaints about the money flowing in, or the dangers of her job. She still refused to have a pimp, though. She kept saying she wasn't going to share her money with any man.

She was certainly good at what she did. Sometimes, I would peek through the keyhole to watch the show. I learned some very unusual things. Things a sixteen year old girl didn't need to know about.

Dee called while I was at Leslies, and I was so glad to hear his voice. As usual, it had been a while since I'd heard from him, and he didn't know about what had been going on. I told him about all the awful things my friends were going through.

He seemed sad about all of it, and when I asked him if I could see him tomorrow, he said he'd meet me at the rec center. Then he asked why he couldn't ever come to my house.

"Because my dad is way too strict. He'll kill any man I date, even when I'm thirty," I replied, rolling my eyes.

Dee laughed nervously, "Well he won't have to worry about me since you told me that. I'll definitely stay away from pops."

We agreed to meet the following day, then I left Leslie's to go home. I had my own chores to take care of still, despite working all day. I finally finished the dishes and threw my exhausted body onto my bed. What a day it had been!

The moment I closed my eyes, the phone rang again. I quickly snatched it up on the first ring, thinking it might be Dee. To my surprise, it was Darnell and he sounded upset at me. I could hear the tension in his voice.

He said that I stood him up that Friday when he was supposed to paint a portrait of me. Then he asked if I still wanted to do it. I told him of course, and that so many things were going on in my life, including the issues with Mecca.

Darnell was upset about the whole thing as well. He told me that he'd known Kyle for a long time, but didn't think he was low-down enough to start messing with Mecca's mother. I told Darnell to change the subject, because every time I thought about Mecca laid up in the hospital bed with an I.V. in her arm, I got angry.

We rescheduled the portrait session for the following Friday, then started talking about the newest movies that were out. He asked if I wanted to see any of them, and if I'd be interested in going with him. I told him I'd let him know for sure.

Truthfully, I was only interested in seeing how Mecca was doing, not any movies. I asked Darnell if he could pick me up early the next morning to see Mecca at the hospital. He said sure, so I gave him directions to pick me up at the rec center. My plan was to visit Mecca, then be back at the rec at six to meet Dee.

I finally prepared for bed. My sisters were watching "Sanford and Son", and were laughing so hard that they didn't notice me remove my diary from its hiding place. I quickly wrote the latest entry, then gathered up my things for a quick bath before bed.

The following morning, I called the hospital to see if Mecca could have visitors. The head nurse at ICU said that they moved her to the Behavioral Health Ward, then gave me the visiting hours.

Ecstatic, I called Avalon with the wonderful news. I told her Darnell would be taking me to hospital and asked if she wanted to come. Avalon declined, saying that she had a counseling session to go to, but would swing by the hospital with Freddie later.

I knocked on my parent's door and called out, asking if it was alright for me to catch the bus to visit Mecca. They yelled back that I could and to grab some money off the end table for bus fare. Everyone in my house was in lazy mode, with no plans to get out of bed yet. On Saturdays, our household didn't get up until around eleven.

Darnell was prompt. He was driving a bad yellow Corvette, and looked good in it. He greeted me, complimenting me on my navy-blue backless dress, then we proceeded to the hospital.

He started making small talk, asking if we could go to his place after the hospital visit. I shrugged nonchalantly, telling him I'd let him know after the visit. Darnell was a nice guy, but he didn't seem like my type. Maybe I would have been all over him if Dee wasn't in the picture.

Darnell was a very educated man, with a head for business. He kept implying that he wanted to settle down and marry a nice lady someday. With a regretful smile, he said that a good woman was the only thing missing from his life.

He pulled into the parking lot of the hospital and parked, telling me that he wasn't going to go in.

"Considering I was with Kyle when she met him…" he shrugged uncomfortably. "I think it's best you go see your friend. Take your time, I'm cool. I've got a really good book to finish anyway."

Darnell pulled out a white book titled "Manchild In the Promised Land", by Claude Brown. I could see he was halfway done with it. He opened the book and started reading, becoming engrossed immediately. I watched him with a tiny smile on my face until he looked up, smiled back, then suggested I get going because my friend needed me.

After entering the hospital, I went to the information desk for directions to the Behavioral Health Ward. I found out where Mecca's room was and rushed off. But before stopping at Mecca's room, I made sure to pick up a card and flowers from the gift shop.

When I knocked on the door, I heard her ask in a mean tone, "Who is it?"

I opened the door and sucked my teeth playfully. "It's Tunisia, girl! Happy as I am to see you, you betta check your tone!"

A big smile engulfed her face, and she even giggled a little. "Girl, I'm so happy to see you, too," she reached out for a hug. "Where's Avalon?"

"Avalon had to have a counseling session, but she said she'd be here later," I answered.

"Girl, bring those flowers over so I can smell them!" she laughed. "I'm so happy you're here. I thought it was my momma coming back."

"Mecca, we don't need to talk about her," I said lightly, putting the flowers in her hands. "I'm here to see you."

She deeply breathed in the fragrance of lilacs, her smile growing even wider. I took them out of her hands and placed them by the window so she could look at them daily. I made some off-hand comment about how there wasn't any herb in the flowers and she didn't need to breathe so deeply. She knew I was joking though, and laughed loudly.

I gave her the card I bought, and told her to read what I had written:

"How can I tell you how thankful I am for the wonderful friend you have always been, Mecca? How can I thank you for the comforting words and caring thoughts you've given me time and time again... and how can I tell you not to take my sunshine away, and that I love you forever and one day... How can I tell you that there is no me without you? How can I tell you that you are a dream that has finally come true?"

Mecca began to cry as she read the card. I hugged her tightly, telling her that everything would be alright. She held me just as tightly, so tight that I almost couldn't breathe. But I understood how she felt: all alone, even when surrounded by people.

She calmed down and started telling me about why she tried to kill herself. I urged Mecca to just put all of that behind her and to continue moving forward. I wanted her to focus on running towards the light, not drowning in darkness again.

I stayed with her for about an hour and a half. When it was finally time for me to leave, I told her I'd be back tomorrow to see her again. That I'd come every day to support her if I had to.

Mecca adopted a blasé tone, "That's cool. You can come tomorrow and as often as you want. Just don't expect me to be here."

I turned to her with an expression of confusion, and she continued with a tiny smirk, "Girl, the doctor said as soon as my momma signs the release papers later today, I'm going home."

My confusion morphed into gladness as a wide smile broke out onto my face. Mecca's smirk was replaced by a genuine smile, and we just stared at each other with matching cheesy grins.

CHAPTER EIGHTEEN

Darnell was so into that book when I got back to his car. He didn't even notice me standing there looking at him. He was a fast reader; he must have finished seven or eight chapters while I was gone. Now it looked like he was almost to the end.

I put my hands on my hips and yelled, "Can you open the door for a lady, Darnell?"

He jumped noticeably, clearly startled. He was deep into the world of 1920's Harlem, but quickly snapped back to 1970's Norfolk, running over to the passenger side door and opening it for me with a warm smile.

I told him the good news: that Mecca was going to be released that day. I was feeling so good about Mecca's recovery that I told Darnell to shoot by his studio. We would finally get that portrait completed.

I thought Dee's car was fast, but Darnell's 'Vette made the Mustang seem like a go-cart. I quickly put on my seatbelt as Darnell took the interstate in the direction of Ocean View, and the condos by the beach.

I was worried about how fast he was driving, though. He was going so fast, the other cars looked like they weren't even moving. I told him to slow down and do the speed limit or take me home.

"No problem," he said, completely at ease. He downshifted and was doing the speed limit in seconds. "We're almost there anyway."

I was surprised that Darnell didn't act put out, and that he respected my wishes. Whenever I asked Dee to slow down, he would ignore me and go even faster. It was like he didn't care that I was scared. But Darnell seemed to care about how I felt over his own feelings.

Minutes later we were turning into a very expensive-looking development. It was a line of white, two-story condos that sat on the beach. I thought to myself what a nice place it was as we ascended a winding staircase to Darnell's penthouse.

Once inside, I could see the ocean from his living room. He caught me staring and told me that on a clear, sunny day he could see as far as the horizon. The furniture was plush and everything was color-coordinated.

His artwork confirmed that he was a very talented artist. Portraits of people, places, and objects covered the walls of his studio. As I admired his works, he invited me to an upcoming art show and said it would be a pleasure to take me.

"I'll get back to you," I said with a friendly smile.

He pulled out his portfolio from one the closets and started showing me some of his best work. His talent was truly out of this world. I wondered what kind of portrait he would produce of me when we were done.

He got all the things he needed and told me to strike a pose. His hands immediately began to move with grace and style. I tried not to move, but it was hard to sit still. I wanted to see what he was drawing!

Every time he caught me peeking, he'd playfully wag his finger at me. I would laugh and say sorry, but he would just reply that I was doing fine. It didn't take him long to complete the portrait, and when I saw the finished product, it took my breath away.

He captured my beauty, vulnerability, and strength all in one setting. My facial expression was pensive. My dark eyes showed traces of pain and wisdom, yet my smile reflected a youthful jubilance.

"It's beautiful!" I breathed in wonder. "Can I keep it? Please?"

"Nope," he shook his head as a boyish smile emerged on his face. "This is mine. If I can't have you in real life, I'll just have to keep you on paper."

I fidgeted uncomfortably, not sure how to explain to him that I was in love with another man. "I don't have any plans of getting involved with someone else. You know I got a dude, so..."

I hated that look of disappointment on his face, but I didn't want him to get any ideas about love or anything. And I definitely didn't want to lead him on, so I told him that I was ready to go.

"I understand," he shrugged, not looking me in the face. Instead, he grabbed the keys to his Corvette, and we were gone.

It was only twelve when Darnell dropped me off at the rec center. He reminded me about the art show and told me to call him if I decided to go. I gave him a friendly hug and promised that I would.

Actually, I really enjoyed being with Darnell for that short period of time. At least he had his own place so that I could chill when I wanted to. Dee, on the other hand, lived in the barracks, and I could never call or see him when I needed him. I was so tired of it. I had suspicions that he may have been married, but I loved and trusted him too much to think about it.

I walked home thinking it was a good day for all of us. I couldn't wait to get inside the house and tell everyone the good news about Mecca. We were surrounded by so much bad news, I wanted something good to shine through for once.

I quickly called Avalon so that I could tell her about Mecca getting released. However, one of her brothers told me that she was in a counseling session, and it should end at two o'clock.

I decided to satisfy my hunger pains, which seemed to be getting worse lately. As I foraged the kitchen for food, the phone rang. I answered quickly, wondering if it was Mecca or Avalon.

Instead, it was Dee, who was calling to make sure I would be at the rec center at six. I assured him I would as picked at some left over collard greens. After we hung up, I saw my mom standing in the doorway frowning.

"You wash your hands, girl? And who was that on the phone?"

"Yes, ma'am, I washed my hands," I lied with a straight face. "And that was Leslie on the phone. She needs me to baby-sit at six."

I breathed a sigh of relief when my mom nodded that it was okay for me to go out, but to make sure I prepared dinner before I left. I knew it was wrong to lie to my parents, but I had to have a way out to see my man.

I carefully made some spaghetti, meatballs, and a tossed salad for my family. It was almost six by the time I finished. Even though I was in a rush, I didn't play when it came to cooking. I hurriedly ran into my room to tell my sisters to set the table because I had to leave.

When I got to the rec center, Dee was leaning against a bicycle rack outside. He saw me coming and motioned for me to get in his car. No hug, no kiss… not even a smile. Just a quick hand gesture telling me what to do.

Finally, he opened the driver's side door and got in. He gave me a kiss on my cheek and neck, probably trying to turn me on. I wasn't really responsive, though. Not because I didn't want him; it was just that my mind was just on all the good things that happened that day.

I guess he could see the joy in my eyes because he asked, "What's goin' on, baby? And how's Mecca?"

"She's gonna get released from the hospital today!" I exclaimed with a big smile.

"That's great," he answered with a wolfish grin. "But I gotta know: was it me that made you so happy or your friend being released today?" I responded by giving him a sweet kiss.

At that point, Dee reached into his glove compartment and pulled out a small mirror. He then reached into his attaché case and produced a white substance. He poured it on the mirror then sniffed it up his nose. He asked me if I wanted to do a line and I quickly said no.

Drugs had ruined Avalon's life. I also saw how drugs had almost killed Mecca. From that point on, I didn't want anything to do with coke, weed, or speed. I was saying no to drugs from that point on.

Dee placed the cocaine back in his case, and as he opened it, I saw various other kinds of drugs inside. I frowned deeply, not knowing that he was into drugs like that. I just thought he smoked herb and did a line every now and then.

With everything that had been happening, I decided it was time to get some stuff off my chest. I was tired, and I told Dee that. I felt ready for a change, but also felt like Dee was keeping me in the same place. It didn't mean that I loved him any less, though. But I was tired, and I told Dee that.

"I'm tired of this whole relationship, Dee," I huffed, crossing my arms over my chest and looking out the window. "I can't ever reach you by phone, and always have to wait for you to call and set up a time for us to meet."

"I told you my situation with the barracks..." he started, but I cut him off.

"Why can't you find a place of your own?" I complained, still refusing to look at him. "Seems like you shoulda been able to by now."

"I told you, I can't afford off-base housing," he answered in an irritable tone. "Yo' ass don't listen."

"Naw, you don't listen," I argued back in an acid-like tone. "But listen to this shit: I'm tired of meeting your way. I need a place to chill, and you don't even care."

"I don't wanna hear any of this shit," he snarled back, but I cut him off again. We were starting to get loud in the car.

"For real, Dee... this relationship is going nowhere and that's because you won't let it. I'm gonna start seeing other dudes, and when I do, it's gonna be your fault."

Dee was really mad at that point. He looked ready to hit something. I hoped it wasn't me, because I wasn't the one to try. After seeing what Leslie went through, I swore that no man would hit me and get away with it. We'd rumble until the sun went down if it came down to it.

He never hit me, though. He just kept cursing me out, calling me stupid, and saying that I was acting immature. That hurt my 16-year-old pride for sure, especially since he didn't know my real age. I always carried myself like an adult around him.

"I don't have time for this.... I got a lot of running to do tonight, Tunisia," he tersely dismissed me. "I'll check you later."

"Cool," I snapped back, slamming the door loudly as I walked off.

I started to head home, but remembered I was supposed to be "baby-sitting" at Leslie's. My irritation with Dee grew even more. My whole night was ruined and I had nothing else planned. I had lied to my mom and dad for nothing. I was fuming as I walked.

Who did he think he was anyway? Talking to me like that when he was the one treating me bad. Calling me stupid and immature, yet he supposedly couldn't even get his own place off the base!

At least I told him what I was going to do. I was definitely going to start messing with other dudes, because I was tired of "just missing" Dee. I needed someone who could be with me when I called, not just when it was convenient for them.

The tears began to form in my eyes and my hearted ached as I walked to Leslie's. Who was I kidding? I was deeply in love with Dee, and couldn't imagine being with anyone else. Even as I walked, I wished that I had Dee next to me.

CHAPTER NINETEEN

The weekend had finally arrived. Leslie wanted me to babysit for her, but I had no intentions of babysitting that night. I hated losing all of that money, but oh well. I had a social life, too.

I told Leslie that Dee was taking me to a house party and arranged for another girl from the 'hood to babysit in my place. Thankfully, Leslie trusted my judgment and agreed to let someone she didn't know watch her precious children.

Avalon came over to my house to fix my hair. She was going to cornrow my hair for the house party. She washed and conditioned it, then put me under the dryer. When my hair was dry, she greased my scalp and started braiding.

Avalon was so talented. She could fix our hair in any style just like professional beauticians. I always told Avalon that she should study cosmetology, but she would just smile and shrug in response.

I was so glad she was off drugs. She had a lot to offer the community, even if she didn't realize it. The amount of money she banked doing other people's hair was proof enough. I was sure she would go places one day.

We began to gossip and reminisce, laughing about things she, Mecca, and I did when we were little kids. We talked about how blessed Mecca was to be alive, then about how blessed we all were to get through our rough times together.

Avalon got quiet for a second, then said in a hesitant tone, "Tunisia, just before Mecca called us that day to tell us she tried to commit suicide, I was going to tell you why I started doing heroin."

"Are you sure you're ready to talk about this?" I asked, gently taking her hands.

"Yeah," she nodded confidently. "I'm ready. Things are finally working out at home since my stepdad agreed to go to a counselor for help."

"Wait a minute... your stepdad? Counseling?" I was very confused.

"Yep," Avalon said, still braiding at a lightning-fast pace. "My momma even stabbed him in the stomach when she found out what was going on."

"Avalon, what are you talking about?" I grabbed her hands to stop her braiding. "Why did your mom stab your dad?"

"Because she found out he had been molesting me since I was nine," she whispered, tears starting to form in her eyes.

"What?!" I exclaimed, jumping to my feet.

"Calm down, T," Avalon put her calm hands on my shoulders.

I was shaking so bad, I wanted to punch a wall or something. I couldn't believe it. Yeah, her dad seemed kind of mean and strict, but I never thought he was capable of something like that. All the times we slept over Avalon's house, all the times we played jump-rope and hop-scotch in front of her house, Avalon was dealing with something very un-childlike.

"Why didn't you tell us, Av?"

"For the same reason I was afraid to tell my mom. If it got back to her, it would kill my mom. She was happy having a man in the house, and I didn't want her to be alone again. You saw what loneliness did to Mecca's mom."

Avalon also admitted that she was ashamed to confess what had been going on. So, she kept it to herself and dealt with it the best way she knew how: escaping the issue. At first it was through her friends, then Freddie, and finally, hard drugs.

"I remember the first time it happened," she told me softly. "Everyone had left to go shopping except for me and him. He came into my room to talk to me, and told me to sit on his lap like I always did.

"This time was different, though," she continued, her tone darkening. "He told me to place my hand on his penis, but I knew that was wrong. So, I jumped off his lap and yelled no."

I pulled Avalon close and wrapped her in a hug as she continued, "He ordered me to sit on his lap again, but that time I said no and tried to run. But before I could get out of the room, he grabbed me and threw me on the bed."

She detailed the entire account, not sparing any horrific details. She told me how he got on top of her and started ripping at her clothing. Avalon kept screaming for him to stop but he started biting and kissing her neck.

He told her, "You better not tell anyone or I'll put your ass out on the street!"

As he was groping her, he kept telling Avalon that it would hurt her mother too much to know what happened, and it would be better if Avalon kept her mouth shut. He also kept threatening her, telling her she better not tell anyone.

"He forced himself on me, and I was only nine. It hurt so bad, but he didn't care. He treated me like an animal for his own sexual pleasure. When he finally finished, he just put his clothes on and walked out, threatening again that I better not tell.

"I was in a state of shock," Avalon continued, her tone hollow. "I could hardly move. I just laid there on my bed, covered in his sweat and a pool of my own blood. When I got up to go clean myself, I hurt everywhere."

Avalon told me that after that first incident, he would come into her room to have sex with her whenever he wanted. It didn't matter how vile the act or how young Avalon was; her stepfather did what he pleased.

After a while, Avalon couldn't look her mother and stepfather in the face. She wanted so badly to tell her mother, but couldn't. What was happening to Avalon was too dark for anyone to know about.

At first, she would be gone from her house as much as possible. I remember when we were younger, Avalon used to always beg to spend the night at my house, or to stay at Mecca's. She never seemed to want to go home, but we thought it was because of the chores and her father's strictness.

Once her dad started keeping her on a shorter leash and not letting her go out as much, Avalon turned to drugs to escape her reality. She told me that when she was on drugs, she felt like she could fly away to another world.

"I kept using drugs to deal with his abuse until Ms. Davies came along," Avalon admitted, finally able to crack a tiny smile. "She knew there was something going on that I was hiding, but never gave up on me. I finally confided in her, and it felt so good. Just like right now."

"What happened then?" I wanted to know.

Avalon finally pulled herself together enough to start braiding my hair again, then answered, "Ms. Davis reported the incident to the authorities. I thought he would go to jail, but he didn't. Ms. Davies told me he would either go to jail or counseling."

"So, he's going to counseling?" I asked in a disgusted voice. I wanted him to be punished, but it seemed like he was getting off easy.

"My mom wanted a divorce, but my stepdad wanted to get some help so all of us could heal. My mom is still having a really hard time dealing with it. I think she hates him now. Mom told me she wished he had died from the stab wound."

Smirking a little, Avalon added, "It felt good to know she was on my side, though. And that she was sorry about it. But seeing her hurting like this… that's the exact reason I didn't tell her in the first place."

Eventually, they were headed for recovery after several counseling sessions. Ms. Davies told them that many families went through that sort of thing, and that the first step to recovery was forgiving the person who wronged you.

"I know you don't agree, T, but we need this," Avalon said confidently. "We need to heal as a family and grow as a family. Nobody's perfect. We're a dysfunctional family like everyone else, but with the right help and guidance..."

"And God," I interjected.

"And God, of course," she added with a laugh. "We're gonna be able to function as a family again. I have faith."

Suddenly, it seemed like a storm well burst inside of her and tears were gushing like crazy. I was familiar with that kind of weeping and knew that Avalon's soul was being healed. She was purging all of the badness to make room for the good.

I stayed quiet and just let her cry. Without saying anything, she got up and went into the bathroom. She stayed there for at least ten minutes. I could hear her sobbing quietly in there, too.

When she finally came out, I immediately said, "Avalon, this wasn't your fault, and it wasn't your mom's fault. This was all your stepdad. What he did was wrong, and he knew it. That's probably why he wants counseling."

She smiled in agreement, still wiping stray tears from her cheeks. Though her eyes were red and puffy from crying, she expertly finished my hair, her hands moving as if they had a mind of their own.

When Avalon finished, I was very pleased with what I saw in the mirror. I looked just like an African princess. I couldn't stop patting my hair and raving about how wonderful it looked. I hugged my friend tightly, thanked her, and told her I'd continue praying for her.

"I appreciate it, girl," she said, hugging me back. "But I gotta go now. Freddie is waiting for me."

I looked out my window and watched Avalon greet Freddie with a kiss. He wrapped her in a big bear hug, causing her to dissolve into giggles. Avalon turned and smiled happily at me. When she took Freddie's hand and walked off, we both knew in that moment that she would be okay.

CHAPTER TWENTY

Dee was right on time picking me up for the house party. He arrived at nine o'clock on the dot, just like he promised. He was looking so good in his red suit with matching tie. He even had a large red brim. I just wanted to eat him up.

I didn't wear a hat because I wanted to show off my cornrows. But I liked how my white pant suit complemented his red. We looked really good standing next to each other, and I rarely left his side once we hit the party.

Dee told me the house belonged to one of his associates, but we weren't going to stay long. I didn't mind. It wasn't too long before they started passing out drugs. Some people were free-basing, others were dropping acid, and some were getting tore up off of weed, liquor, and cocaine.

I refused to take any drugs that night. After everything that had happened to my friends, I knew that addiction could happen even to me. I let the coke pass by, the acid, the herb... all of it. Dee kept asking me to take some, but I always turned down the offer. I wanted to become drug-free.

Barry White was sounding good, and I started dancing with a cute brother in a dark blue suit when a woman in a red outfit marched through the front door. She was about five-foot three and looked kind of familiar.

She immediately started scanning the party for someone, and the moment she saw Dee, she angrily stormed over to him. Some people stopped dancing to watch. The look on her face said something was about to go down.

Dee jumped off the couch in shock. "What are you doing here?"

The woman glared back, "My friend Thelma is at this party. She told me to come and see what your black ass was doing."

Dee became very defensive, waving his hands back and forth. "It's not like that, baby."

"Then how is it?" she snapped back.

"She's just a friend of mine," he answered, his voice stammering. I'd never seen him look so nervous.

That woman wasn't having it, though. "Well, speaking of this little friend… where the hell is she? And don't lie, 'cuz I'm on to you!"

Dee was trying to get out of trouble by using his sweet talk and affectionate ways. It always worked on me, but I guess this lady was immune to it.

Before he could smooth her ruffled feathers, she pushed his hand away. "Don't even try that shit. I know you're running around on me. At first, I wasn't sure, but luckily Thelma called me tonight to tell me you showed up at the party with some trampy-looking thing in a white suit."

With a voice as hard and cold as steel, she threatened, "Don't play with me, motherfucker. For the last time, where is she?"

I looked down at my white suite, a feeling of immense dread settling in my stomach like a brick. Uh-oh. They were talking about me. And what was this woman talking about, saying Dee was running around on her? Did that mean….?

No, it couldn't be. Dee swore he was single. I looked at the lady in red and saw her standing next to her friend, who was talking and pointing at me. The lady in red got a threatening look on her face and approached me.

"Look girl," she cut her eyes at me, "what the hell are you doing with my husband?"

Husband?!? Oh, Lord… I didn't know what to do. Watching this angry woman in front of me, an array of emotions suddenly washed over me. Hurt, anger, but most importantly… fear. A lot of fear. This lady had a look in her eye that clearly said this confrontation was not over.

My legs were like jelly, my mouth felt like sand. I had an eerie, yet familiar feeling in my stomach. That same feeling you have when you know you're about to get into a fight, but really don't want to.

Dee finally came over. "Baby, just go home."

She looked at him like he was crazy. "Go to hell, motherfucker."

Dee grabbed her arm and tried to pull her away, but she reached up and slapped the hell out of him. The slap was so loud that the music literally stopped, record scratch and all. By this time, everyone in the party was watching the confrontation.

Infuriated and hurt, Dee's wife started calling him all kinds of names. Then she started slapping and punching him, like a demon had taken over her. He kept blocking her blows and trying to hug her, but she pushed him away.

Eyes flashing, she reached into her purse and pulled out a .38 caliber pistol. When she did that, everyone started yelling and stampeding to get to the door first. And I was retreating right along with them!

I ran out the front door at top speed. I didn't know where I was, or where I was going, but I kept running. I looked back once (bad habit of mine), and the last thing I saw was Dee's wife firing a shot at him. The bullet hit Dee in the leg and he instantly dropped to the floor with a yell.

I was not fazed, though. I was too busy running for my life. I was out of breath and wanted to stop, but I was scared. I didn't have my friends with me, and no one knew where I was.

I looked back again to see where Dee's wife was. To my horror, she was right behind me, that pistol still flashing in her right hand. I was so terrified; I almost stumbled and fell. Thankfully, God was on my side and I was able to increase me speed. She still had me in her line of sight, though.

I was coming around a corner and saw a police car approaching from up the street. I was so relieved. The cop car was about four blocks away, but at least it was coming my way. Maybe someone at the party had called the police, but I was just glad to have a little help.

I also heard the sirens from the ambulance. I knew it was for Dee, but I didn't dare go back to see how he was. Everything was happening so fast, I just wanted to get away.

How did this happen anyway? I should have known he was married! And Hell hath no fury like a woman scorned. All of that had to be a setup. Dee's wife and her friend probably knew he'd been messing around for a long time, and planned the whole thing. They were trying to kill two birds with one stone, and I was one of those birds!

Well, I was flying as fast as a dove, that's for sure. I quickly turned the corner and saw the police car speed up. I jumped out right in front of the police car, which screeched to a halt to avoid running me over.

"Is there a problem, ma'am?" the officer asked, walking up to me.

Before I had the chance to answer, there was a gunshot, then he dropped to the ground, screaming in pain. It was Dee's wife who shot the gun, and the bullet pierced the cop's shoulder. I knew that was a bullet meant for me, though.

The fallen officer's partner drew his own gun and pointed it at her, yelling "Freeze right where you are! Throw down your weapon!"

At first, she didn't comply. She was out of control, screaming, crying, and calling Dee a low-down, dirty dog. I had matching feelings and was thinking the exact same thing. But instead of arguing with cops like her, I chose to hide behind their car.

The officer still had his gun drawn, and called for immediate backup. I started thinking he was going to shoot her, but then Dee's wife finally threw down her gun. Another two squad cars arrived, and two officers jumped out. They roughly tackled Dee's wife to the ground and arrested her immediately.

Police cars and paramedics were coming from everywhere, mainly because an officer was injured. I was standing in the middle of the street, my eyes accosted in every direction by red and blue lights.

One ambulance took the wounded officer, the other one transported Dee.

I, on the other hand, was placed in the back of a cop car. They said they needed to take me to the station for questioning. They also said they'd have to notify my parents after finding out that I was only sixteen.

The policeman who had Dee's wife at gunpoint told me later that she was being charged with possession of an unregistered firearm, felony assault on a police officer, two counts of attempted murder, as well as other charges.

CHAPTER TWENTY-ONE

By the time the officers brought me back to the 'hood, they had already notified my parents about the incident. And boy, were my parents irate! I knew I was gonna get it. I had half a mind to beg the cops to stay and protect me.

My parents yelled and cursed me out like they'd never done before. They fussed at me simultaneously, their voices merging into a loud blend of parental anger. Then my dad yelled at me while my mom shook her head disappointedly. Afterwards, she yelled while my dad went and got the belt.

"You are too damned grown, girl!" My mom shouted at me, "Don't you know a hard head makes a soft ass? I better not ever catch you with that grown man again! And he's married?!? What the hell is wrong with you?"

"Ma, I didn't know he was married," I tried to argue back weakly, but my mom looked at me like I was the dumbest person on Earth.

"I don't want to hear it," she said through gritted teeth. "I'm done with you. I'ma let your father handle this."

"But ma-!" I started to protest.

"Not another word!" she roared at me as my father returned with a thick belt.

That night, I got the worst whupping of my life. Not only that, but I was on punishment indefinitely. With one final swipe at my butt, my dad ordered me to my room, telling me that my grown little ass better be there when he came in to check on me, and that I would never know when that was.

When I went to my room, I was out of it. I didn't pay attention to my sisters; I just cried and cried. I was so hurt… and angry! I couldn't believe Dee had done this to me. The entire eight months, he was just using me.

Every time I thought about it, my rage multiplied. He had the best of both worlds. He had a wife at home to cook for him, clean up after him, then lay in bed with him all night after making love.

But he also had me: the hot, young fling on the side that he could use to get away from his married life. He could run around with me pretending to be single, not having to adhere to the rules his wife put down. Like that "curfew" his barracks had...

He had his cake and ate it, too... and then he had nothing. It served him right as far as I was concerned. His selfishness caused a lot of unnecessary pain and confusion. I could have lost my life because of him!

How could he do this to me? We had dreams. He said we were going to get married and have dozens of children. What a fool I was. He was already married. For all I knew, he could've already had kids.

I loved and trusted him. I trusted him so much that I never worried about getting pregnant because I believed he would be there for me. I thought we would be there for each other. Well, he didn't have to worry about seeing me anymore. I never wanted to see his face again in my life.

I was hungry as usual again, so I went into the kitchen to see what was in the pot on the stove. I didn't care what it was; I just needed to get some food in me. It seemed like lately I was always in the kitchen.

When the phone rang, I answered it, assuming it would be a family member. My mom had been calling her sisters all night to tell them about how the cops had brought me home, how I'd been caught up with a married man, and how his wife tried to kill me.

However, it was Dee on the phone. I frowned and immediately started to put the phone back in the cradle. That is, until I heard his pleading voice. I put the phone back to my ear, but refused to say anything.

"Please don't hang up on me, baby..."

I merely sucked my teeth in response. I was not his baby anymore.

"Please, just hear me out," he begged. "I just needed to talk to you. To hear your voice. I was worried about you, baby. I saw her chasing you out with that gun... I was scared."

In a softer voice he said, "And I know you were scared for me. I know you still care about me. I'm okay, though. The bullet just grazed my leg. The doc had to put a few stitches in, but I'm alright."

I rolled my eyes, unable to believe he was talking like that on the phone. I almost died, and here he was trying to sweet talk me like he was doing his wife earlier.

"Dee, I'm glad you're okay, but we're through," I stated firmly. "I never want to see or hear from you again."

"It's not over, baby," he pleaded. "We had dreams, remember? It's not over with us. Please... let me drive over to explain. She's nothing to me."

"She's your wife," I barked back, finally at my wit's end. "And don't bother driving over here. I already told you that I never want to see you again. And I mean never."

"I can't do that, baby," he said over the phone, his voice breaking. "Let me at least see how you're doing. I'm worried about you."

"You need to be worried about your wife," I snapped back. "She's in jail because of how low-down you are. You are a dirty dog!"

"I love you, not her…" he started to say but I hung up on him.

He was still lying and talking when I put the phone on the cradle. I was over it all and just wanted to go to bed. I put the lids back on the pots and went to my room. I couldn't even eat anymore. I had totally lost my appetite. I was angry, sad, and completely disgusted with men at that point.

I looked in the metal box where I kept letters and poems that Dee had given to me. One of the poems he copied was from a sonnet written by Elizabeth Barrett Browning. My eyes welled with tears as I skimmed some of the lines:

"How do I love thee? Let me count the ways. I love thee to the depth and breadth of height.... I love thee to the level of everyday's Most quiet need, by sun and candlelight. I love thee freely as men strive for Right… and, if God choose, I shall love thee better after death."

After skimming the sonnet three times, I finally let quiet sobs escape from my body. I had mixed emotions about the whole ordeal. The words of the sonnet were pure and true, but they had been given to me by a man who was a liar. Everything was a life.

I was going under. Despite being so angry with him, I still loved him. My heart still ached for him, for what could have been. Even after everything that had happened, I already missed those good times with Dee.

I placed the sonnet back in the box and looked up at the calendar on my dresser. I smiled softly as I thought of all the wonderful things we experienced together. I reminisced on how long we had been going out.

Then I started thinking about something else. Fear came over me, and my body began to tremble. On impulse, I got up and snatched the calendar off the dresser. I frantically started counting the days.

I counted again and again and again, thinking maybe I made a mistake. The numbers would come out right; I just needed to make them come out right. But no matter how many times I added up the boxes on the calendar, the message was the same.

I began to worry. When was the last time I had my period? I didn't see it last month or the month before that one. Then I thought about how hungry I'd been lately. What if I was pregnant? There was no way I was bringing a married man's baby into this world.

I decided to check it out and confirm my fears. I ditched school the next morning and went to the clinic to take a pregnancy test. I didn't tell Mecca or Avalon about what was going on, even though they confided in me about everything.

I arrived at the clinic at about nine-thirty, and the nurses took me into a room to ask me some questions. I filled out all the forms, asking if they were going to tell my parents. The nurse informed me that the exam itself was confidential, but any follow up would require parental notification.

I went into the exam room and was looked at by a friendly-looking doctor. After taking a urine sample from me, he advised that the results would take about three days. He told me they would call with the results, which meant I would have to beat my parents to the phone.

The three days I waited for the results dragged by, but the entire time I prayed that I wasn't carrying Dee's baby. I threw up every morning of those three days, but I kept telling myself that it was just nerves, not morning sickness.

I will never forget that day the clinic called me. They confirmed my suspicions, telling me that I was seven weeks pregnant. I remember feeling like I was falling, then dropping the phone in shock.

I cried constantly, unable to believe this was happening to me. But it was. There was no running from it, no pretending like this wasn't real. That entire week I was quiet and depressed, and my friends couldn't figure out what was wrong. I was going under.

At least Mecca was adjusting well at home. She told us that she was trying to forgive her mother for what had happened. Mecca and her mom grew closer than ever, mainly because Kyle was gone.

After Mecca tried to kill herself, he left and never came back. We didn't think it was Mecca's mom that kicked him out; we think he left on his own. Rumor had it that he was seeing some young girl in our 'hood. He sure was a dog.

Even Avalon seemed to be doing well. Her entire family started attending church and getting involved in community projects. And they would still go to the counseling center for support.

It seemed like everyone had gone through dark times and emerged victorious. Everyone except for me…

CHAPTER TWENTY-TWO

I was still depressed about being pregnant, and I hadn't even told my parents yet. I didn't want to imagine what kind of whupping I'd get after dropping that bomb. Life was so dark for me at the time, I needed my own escape. So, I decided to turn on the television.

I hadn't watched TV in a few days, and immediately started channel surfing for something good. I noticed that our park was on the news. They were reporting a stabbing that had occurred earlier in the day.

The news reporter went on to say that the victim was a woman that had two young children. I sat up to pay closer attention, then screamed when Leslie's picture flashed across the scene. I dropped to my knees, asking God why such horrible things were happening.

The reporter went on to say that the woman was found dead on arrival. Then they showed a picture of Mo Joe, announced that he was her husband and the prime suspect of the brutal murder. Mo Joe was still at large, with the police asking for any witnesses and offering a reward for his capture.

"Lord, no… it can't be," I cried over and over.

It had happened, this was real. It was on the radio, television, and even in the newspaper. I just couldn't believe it. Stabbings, shootings, and other crimes occurred where I lived, but this was the first time it happened to someone I was actually close to. Someone who was almost like family.

I cried for Leslie. I cried for her children. I even cried for Mo Joe. Everyone was already accusing Mo Joe and trying to convict him. He hadn't even been arrested or gone to trial yet.

And though Leslie and Mo Joe fought all the time, I didn't believe he was the one who stabbed her. He was violent, but I had seen men do worse to her. To this day, I still believe that it was one of Leslie's johns that murdered her.

The phone rang, and it was Dee. I immediately hung up, not wanting to get dragged into a conversation with him. I definitely didn't want him to know I was carrying his baby. And I had too much on my mind with Leslie's murder.

I quickly called Mecca and Avalon to talk to them about the murder. Both of them agreed that it was sad how women got battered and killed every day, yet it seemed like nobody did anything about it.

After a lot of thought, prayer, and crying, I finally confronted my mother about my pregnancy. She told me that I should keep the baby, but I adamantly told her I had no intentions of bringing that child into the world. I didn't want my child growing up without a father, being the bastard child of a married man.

My mother and I argued about it for hours. She kept saying that I made my bed and needed to lie in it. When I repeated that I was having an abortion, she yelled that she wasn't going to sign any papers for the procedure or take me to get it done.

My mother was very religious and completely against abortion. In her eyes, it was murder, pure and simple. So, I argued a hypothetical situation: what if someone was raped? Should they have to carry a rapist's baby?

Mother told me that I wasn't raped, and I should carry the baby for nine months then give it up for adoption. She said that there were many women out there who couldn't have children and would feel blessed to adopt my baby.

I was only sixteen, though, and I wasn't trying to hear it. Finally, I threatened her that if she didn't take me to get it done, I would have to go to one of the illegal, dangerous clinics. She saw in my eyes that I was serious, and I could see the fear take over her eyes.

We weren't in agreement over the life of my unborn child, but we were in agreement over one life: mine. And my mother didn't want to lose me on the dirty operating table of an illegal abortion doctor.

CHAPTER TWENTY-THREE

So, I speak to you now, Aja, my beautiful child, in an attempt to warn you not to grow up too fast. It was a hard struggle for all of us years ago, and we still have many problems yet to resolve. But with love, laughter, literature, and wisdom we can communicate with our children, and pass along positive ideas to the next generation.

Aja, if I can help you be a wiser teenager, then you will mature into a wise adult. The problems Mecca, Venice, Avalon, Leslie and I had were real and ugly. And although it is emotionally and psychologically difficult for me to dig up the atrocities of the past, if it can bring healing and hope to the present, then it is worth it.

My daughter looked at me with the typical smirk of a know-it-all 15-year-old. "Ma, I'm glad we're close and all, but things are different now. What you're talking 'bout was way back in the day. I mean, really? Eight tracks? Things aren't like they were when you were growing up."

I laughed loudly, thinking of how much she sounded like me when I was her age. However, she was the spitting image of her father, and my husband, Darnell. She even had his artistic flair.

"Aja," I admonished her gently, "haven't you been listening to my story? The more things change, the more they stay the same."

"I dunno," she disagreed playfully. "I mean, it seemed safer back then. People don't just casually do lines of coke. And we definitely don't stick our thumbs out for no rides. Hitchhiking is so eighties."

We shared a laugh, then I hit her with The Look. The one I learned from my own mother. The look that guaranteed your child would be compelled to tell you the truth when you asked an important question.

"*So* eighties, huh? Let me ask you this, Ms. We-Don't-Hitchhike-Cuz-It's-Played-Out… have you ever jumped in a car with a guy after knowing him for a few minutes? Let's say, after hanging out at the mall or at the movies or something?"

Aja grinned sheepishly. I could tell she was tempted to lie, but The Look never failed, especially when she saw my knowing smile. She matched my grin, and I marveled at how much she resembled Darnell.

"Ma..." she complained. "It's really not the same. I mean, yeah... me and my friends may meet some guys. Then if we all decide we wanna go somewhere else, we get a ride with them. It's not the same as hitchhiking."

"The hell it isn't," I drawled, piercing her with my sternest gaze. "Think about what happened to Venus. It can also happen to you. Just because you've been hanging out with this person, they're still a stranger to you, Aja. And they can just as easily take you somewhere you don't want to go, and make you do things you don't want to do."

Aja's dubious look compelled me to add, "Aja, nothing has changed with time. Not even the 'nothing bad can happen to me' attitude of the young. I know because I was that way, my mother was that way, and so on. When we're young, we believe we're invincible."

"It's not that, ma," she laughed. "It's just that we've been educated different than y'all. We were taught about drugs and sex and all that at a young age. We were taught that stuff while we were still in school. And we travel in groups, not alone."

"And you slowly build up that idea that nothing bad will happen to you," I nodded. "It starts with one small risk, one stupid little mistake that you don't suffer any repercussions for. Then you get bolder and step out even more. It happens to everyone, Aja."

I put on the best "naïve teenager" persona I could muster, and impersonated her with wide-eyes (and bad grammar), "What? Me? What I need to be careful for? Nah... no way! I'm different, yo. I'm smarter, yo. I know better. I know the streets... I'm street smart, son. Ain't nothin' happened yet, so what's one more time?"

I gazed knowingly at my daughter, who wore an embarrassed expression on her face. I had her down to a "T". I was sure that at some point or another, she uttered those very same phrases before going out to do something stupid. I was just blessed that she hadn't been hurt.

I went on to explain to her how I married Darnell after that mess with Dee. After the abortion, I was going under, drowning in depression, negativity, and a newfound resentment of men.

"It was your father that pulled me out, Aja. He comforted me and gave me love the best way he knew how. And he was respectful. I was still underage and not allowed to court men. That man waited two years for me. He took the time to help me heal, then built a friendship with me before he made any moves."

I told her about Avalon, and how she had been getting sicker after I fell into my depression. The illness was unknown then, but now the medical field has changed enough where we have more information, more cases, more evidence.

Avalon had AIDS. We found out that she contracted it from sharing needles with other drug users. Doctors said the HIV virus could be carried for ten to fifteen years before it turned into full-blown AIDS.

"So... where's Avalon now? It's weird that I've never met her," Aja asked.

With a deep, painful sigh, I answered, "Honey, Avalon died from AIDS three years ago. She paid the ultimate price for the choices she made. She chose drugs to deal with her abuse, and it cost her life."

Teenage girls are often perceived as being helpless and unassuming. There are certain men who abuse women that appear to be weak. But even women who are physically and mentally strong but emotionally weak get abused as well. Someone may be strong in one area, but weak in another.

Abuse can be emotional, physical, or sexual. It can even be a combination of all three. The number of shelters and outreach programs that assist battered and abused women has increased over the past 20 years.

Despite the increase in reported cases, more women are courageously seeking help and speaking out now. And more women and men are speaking out against domestic violence and other forms of abuse. It is time to be concerned with the prevention of abuse.

One way to accomplish this is by studying the abusers. They need to be educated and counseled about their "trigger buttons". In other words, the things that trigger their abusive behavior. They need to be taught healthy methods to deal with anger in a non-violent, non-abusive manner.

Another way of prevention is education. We need to understand that abuse isn't just men on women; it can be women on men as well. It can also be women and men abusing children, who then grow up learning to be abusers of their loved ones.

We need to educate young boys and girls at an early age that abuse is wrong. Whether you are abusing someone else or receiving it, young children need to be educated on how to identify it, and how to seek help.

Parents, preachers, and teachers need to step in and take a more educational role in this area. If we can teach at a younger and younger age that abuse is wrong and it is a crime, we could significantly reduce abuse cases.

We also need our lawmakers to pass stricter laws, with tougher abuse penalties. Tougher punishment for the perpetrators would serve as a deterrent when teaching young children that abuse is a very serious crime. We must let our lawmakers know how serious we are about passing tougher laws.

Not to mention, volunteering at a women's shelter or halfway house has an amazing effect on our community. Not only are you contributing a positive, loving energy to someone who needs it, you are also opening yourself up to more education. When we offer our help from the base level and work up, not only are we able to teach others, but we ourselves learn more about abuse from the stories of others.

Darnell had been up in the attic cleaning and gathering items for the Salvation Army while I was chatting with Aja. He stumbled into the kitchen with an armful of items, then called for me to help him before something dropped.

As I reached for a large canvas that was slipping, that boyish smile of his emerged again as he said, "Tunisia, look at what you're holding. I found that in the attic! Can't believe it held up after all these years. Do you remember when I painted this portrait of you?"

I looked at the colorful canvas, then up at my wonderful husband. "Of course, I do. You painted that picture years ago in your penthouse in Ocean View. As a matter of fact, that was the first portrait of many that you did for me."

Darnell and I shared a loving gaze and a long kiss before Aja interjected, "Y'all are like two teenagers sometimes. Daddy," she whined, "you're interrupting me and mom's 'girl talk'."

"Well excuse me for trying to be smooth and romantic with my wife," he laughed, mussing her hair as he walked out.

Aja looked at me and asked, "Mom, how does a woman know if she is in need of support or help?"

I responded, "If your partner hits, slaps, chokes, bites, punches, cuts, burns, or spits on you, that is abuse. If they insult you, call you names, restrain you against your will, humiliate you, stop you from seeing your friends and family, then you are experiencing abuse.

"Unfortunately, it often starts off subtle, with controlling actions perceived as someone caring about you. But it's abuse. If your partner destroys your property or anything emotionally personal to you... if they restrict your access to money or even monitor your phone calls, if they lie to you in order to manipulate you, or make promises to control you, that is abuse.

"If they force you to do any sexual acts... anything you don't want to do... that is abuse. Your body is just that: yours. No one has the right to claim your body as theirs and force you to do something sexually that you don't want. Even if it's your boyfriend or husband."

I cannot tell another woman what to do, I can only offer advice, just like I tried to do when I was a young, foolish teenager. Back then, I didn't know much about life and did the best I could when it came to giving guidance. Now, I have much more life experience, good and bad.

If Leslie had pressed charges and gotten a protective order against Mo Joe, maybe she would still be alive today. Maybe she wouldn't have had to move so much, and could have held a regular job instead of prostituting.

Maybe her life would have taken a different turn. We'll never know.

If you find yourself in this situation, contact the authorities immediately. If nothing else, confide in a loved one. You may get angry at them for intervening, but the more family members and friends that know about what you're going through, the more support you have when it's time to get help.

What it comes down to is respect and love. Brothers and sisters, love one another. Respect one another. Truly cherish one another. Then grow with one another.

Fixing my daughter with The Look again, I said, "Now Aja, I've talked enough and it's my turn to listen. Tell me what's going on in your life?"

EPILOGUE

The following is a list of helpful options that I highly recommend to anyone who has been abused.

1. Call 911. It is important to have a legal record of the abuse. Police intervention can lead to an arrest, and hopefully, future counseling.
2. If you are injured, seek medical attention and make sure you keep copies of the treatment and photographs of your injuries. Some states automatically take pictures when a battery report is filed, but in case your state or local authorities do not practice that police, make someone documents the injuries.
3. Call the National Domestic Violence Hotline at 1-800-700-SAFE (7233) or visit www.thehotline.org.
4. Leave an unsafe situation and find a shelter or stay with a family member or friend. If you want assistance finding a safe house, the number listed above can help.
5. If and when you do leave the abuser, gather important papers and documentation so that you have no reasons to go back to where the abuser is.

My publisher's website contains contact information so that you can write me and tell me what is on your heart. I will do my best to offer sound, positive guidance, and if I cannot give you the assistance you need, I have access to a qualified group of caring, professional counselors and therapists who will volunteer their time to help you.

I realize there are many young ladies out there who would like to have someone to talk to or need to share things that are deeply buried in their hearts. Maybe you have been the victim of rape. Perhaps you had an abortion and are having a difficult time dealing with the guilt or shame. If you need someone to talk to, I'm here.

Maybe you are depressed and cannot afford a counselor. Maybe you have a drug problem and need someone to talk to. Perhaps you know someone who is depressed or has a drug problem. If so, contact me or feel free to give them a copy of this book as a gift and tell them to contact me, or someone who can help them.

Young men and women, you are our future. I want you to know that we care about you and want to help you reach your full potential.

ABOUT THE AUTHOR

Joyce Mayo was born to a military family in South Carolina and grew up in Virginia. She has received a Bachelor of Science degree in Criminal Justice from Old Dominion University. She also attended Norfolk State University, with a focus on early childhood education, where she received her teaching credentials. She taught in the public school system for over ten years and continues to volunteer her services for her community and church, including working in a shelter for abused women in Chesapeake, VA.

She is the author of "Abused and Abandoned", "Too Late To Turn Back", and "Love Guides Me", all currently available on Amazon and Barnes & Noble.

Her first children's book, "A, E, I, O, U and Sometimes Y: The Short Vowel Friends", will be available in the spring of 2021. She plans to release a series of children's books to encourage beginning readers with fun sounds and bright, funny characters.

Joyce spends her days gardening, writing, and enjoying retirement. She also advocates strongly for domestic violence awareness and support for war veterans.

Further information on how you can help someone suffering from abuse or PTSD is prominently showcased on the TaevoPublishing.com website. You can also find out more about her and her upcoming projects.

She currently lives a quiet life in eastern Virginia with her daughter – who is also her publisher – and her grandchildren.

BE SURE TO CHECK OUT THE EXCITING SEQUEL, *TOO LATE TO TURN BACK* AND SEE WHAT TUNISIA, AVALON, AND MECCA MADE ON THEIR HEALING JOURNEYS!

NOW AVAILABLE ON ALL PLATFORMS AND THE PUBLISHER'S WEBSITE:

WWW.TAEVOPUBLISHING.COM

Made in the USA
Monee, IL
10 November 2021